Pierce Rinkon lives a simple life. Having been born with a learning disorder as well as a disability, he knew he was considered by most to be a little on the dim side. That doesn't stop him from enjoying his life, though. His work as a receptionist for his small town's sheriff's office allows him plenty of interaction with others. For fun, Pierce runs, boxes, and finds men interested in a quick romp. After all, he doesn't expect anyone to be interested in him long-term. While out on a morning run deep in the woods, he spots an old acquaintance — retired deputy Mac. When Pierce heads over to say hi, he watches something crazy happen . . . an animal changes into a man. As he's struggling to process what he's seen, a good-looking dark-haired guy named Daevon makes it plain he's interested in him. Except, Daevon isn't human, and he turns into a scary-looking wolverine. On top of that, Pierce discovers Daevon is smart, educated, and is a retired college professor. How could Daevon possibly be interested in a dumb, small-town hick like Pierce?

The unauthorized reproduction or distribution of this copyrighted work is illegal. Criminal copyright infringement, including infringement without monetary gain, is investigated by the FBI and is punishable by up to 5 years in federal prison and a fine of $250,000.

This book is a work of fiction. Names, characters, places, and incidents either are products of the author's imagination or are used fictitiously. Any resemblance to actual events or locales or persons, living or dead, is entirely coincidental.

With a Gentle Nudge
Copyright © 2019 Charlie Richards
ISBN: 978-1-4874-2737-5
Cover art by Angela Waters

All rights reserved. Except for use in any review, the reproduction or utilization of this work in whole or in part in any form by any electronic, mechanical or other means, now known or hereafter invented, is forbidden without the written permission of the publisher.

Published by eXtasy Books Inc or
Devine Destinies, an imprint of eXtasy Books Inc

Look for us online at:
www.eXtasybooks.com or www.devinedestinies.com

With a Gentle Nudge
Kontra's Menagerie: Book Twenty-Six

By

Charlie Richards

DEDICATION

A kind heart is a fountain of gladness, making everything in its vicinity freshen into smiles.
~Washington Irving

Chapter One

After shaking out his arms, Pierce Rinkon began unwrapping the tape around his hands. He ignored the sweat dripping down his body as he grinned with pleasure. Spending twenty minutes beating a heavy bag always left him feeling good.

"Great intensity, Pierce," Anthony stated, slapping him on the shoulder. With a laugh, he added, "You always give that heavy bag a hell of a beating. Are you imagining someone you hate?"

Pierce chuckled as he shook his head. Peering down at the slightly shorter man—the gym's owner, Anthony O'Dair—he admitted, "Pretty much my mind goes blank. All I think about is how I need to move my body."

Anthony patted Pierce's shoulder again, continuing to grin widely. "There's an opening in the boxing tournament next Saturday." Resting his hands on his hips, Anthony told him, "I know you'd originally declined, but I thought I'd check with you first to see if your schedule opened up."

Placing his unwrapped boxing tape in the garbage, Pierce considered Anthony's question. He'd competed in a number of competitions at the gym over the last couple of years, and he normally did pretty well, even managing to win a few. Unfortunately, over the last several months, some new gym members had become extremely competitive.

Pierce didn't enjoy sparring with them because they were so aggressive. The trio boxed with each other and any guys bigger than themselves that they could talk into it. They seemed to want to make a point that they could take out all the boxers larger than themselves.

The jerks have a size inferiority complex.

Having made the mistake of accepting what Pierce had thought was a friendly sparring match, he'd learned his lesson first hand. At six-foot-four, he'd had a good height advantage on Kenny, who stood at six-foot-even. However, since Kenny and his friends focused on pumping up their arms, the other man was wider than Pierce. Uncertain what to expect, Pierce had started out keeping his punches light as he felt out his opponent.

Hearing Kenny's buddies—Bill and Stan—shouts of encouragement to, "Take him down, lay him out, and put him down," told Pierce it wasn't going to be a friendly match. Kenny had tried to wale on Pierce, but Pierce had been boxing for years. He'd picked up his game and landed enough punches to send Kenny to his knees, getting himself out of the ring as swiftly as possible.

As it was, Pierce had been damn sore for days.

Kenny had asked for a rematch a week later, but so far, Pierce had been able to put him off. He didn't accept fights from Bill or Stan, either. The trio razzed him often, asking him what he was afraid of and jeering him for being *yella*.

Whatever. I don't need to prove myself to anyone.

Pierce boxed for fun.

"So what do you say?" Anthony asked, redrawing Pierce's attention.

Do I want to possibly box one of the annoying trio?

Not really, but Pierce realized he couldn't allow a few assholes to drive him away from one of his favorite pastimes. Besides, with the different weight divisions, Pierce hoped it wouldn't happen. He knew there was a chance, however, since even though the trio were slightly shorter than him, they were heavy with muscle.

Dumb 'roid heads.

"Yeah. I'll fill the slot," Pierce stated, meeting Anthony's gaze. Curiosity getting the better of him, he asked, "Who dropped out?"

"Fantastic. I'll go get the forms while you clean up and change." Anthony grinned broadly as he began walking backward toward his office. "And Kenny had to withdraw after cracking a couple bones in his left hand." Snorting, Anthony rolled his eyes. "I don't know what he decided to punch, but he's paying for it now."

"Huh. Okay." Pierce waved and started toward the locker room. At least one of the three wasn't going to be competing.

While Pierce didn't like wishing ill on anyone, he couldn't say he was sorry about feeling a sense of relief.

Pierce opened his locker and pulled out a towel. After stripping down, he wrapped it around his waist before shoving the dirty clothes into his bag. He grabbed his shower kit and headed to the showers.

As Pierce reached into a stall and turned on the water, he felt a smack to his ass. He scowled as he peered over his shoulder. Seeing Bill standing there in his workout gear, an unfriendly gleam in his brown eyes, Pierce bit back a sneer and smoothed his face into a bland expression.

"Bill," Pierce stated by way of greeting.

"Hey, cocksucker," Bill responded glibly. "Overheard you're takin' Kenny's place in the contest."

Pierce dipped his chin in a slight nod. "Yep." He didn't know if Bill truly knew he was gay, but he wasn't going to engage. That would just encourage the man. "See you there."

Turning back toward his shower, Pierce stepped into the stall. As he pulled the curtain closed, he heard Bill call, "Glad ta hear it." Then Bill's voice lowered, turning mean. "Can't wait to get a shot at knockin' out a butt-muncher like you."

Gritting his teeth, Pierce hung up his towel and pulled out his soap. As he washed, he thought about reporting Bill's comment to Anthony. Pierce didn't advertise the fact that he was gay, and neither did the gym owner.

Pierce knew Anthony swung his way because he'd noticed the way the guy had sprung a boner while watching him change in the locker room once. Thinking the gym owner pretty fine, he'd offered to share a little fun. That had been three years before, and every once in a while, they hooked up for some mutual satisfaction.

Over the years, Pierce had created a number of similar deals with guys in and around town. None of them were interested in a relationship. Besides, even if they were, Pierce had no delusions that one of them would want to deal with Pierce's issues permanently.

While Pierce could learn just about anything, it took him longer. School had been brutal. Not only did he have the stigma of being a dumb jock with dyslexia, but he also had to overcome slight brain damage caused by his mother doing drugs while she was pregnant.

Good thing my father is such a kind and patient man.

Although he still worries about why I choose to be punched on a regular basis.

Finishing his shower, Pierce decided to give a friendly warning to Anthony. His fuck-buddy deserved to know that some of his customers were homophobes. He knew his friend was deep in the closet. Anthony didn't want his sexual orientation to impact his business.

Pierce dried swiftly, then slung the damp towel back around his waist. Carrying his shower supplies, he returned to his locker. He spotted Anthony waiting for him, a clipboard in hand.

"I filled out everything for you, so you just need to sign the bottom," Anthony told him softly after a glance around. "Figured it'd be easier for you."

Smiling in appreciation, Pierce murmured, "Thanks, Anth." Then he swept his gaze over the space, too, before opening his locker. Lowering his voice further, he whispered, "Wanted to warn you. Bill is a homophobe." Seeing the way Anthony's brows shot up in obvious question, Pierce added, "He's said some shit to me."

Anthony's face paled a little. "How the hell would he even know about you?"

Pierce shrugged his wide shoulders. "No idea." The gym had been his safe place, but that seemed to be changing. "Just thought I'd give you a heads up."

Taking the clipboard, Pierce stared at the form on it. He took in the lines that formed boxes and the letters that were supposed to be words. Pierce took a deep breath and let it out slowly.

The more worked up he was, the harder it was for him to comprehend what he was seeing.

"You just need to sign here." Anthony pointed near the bottom.

Pierce nodded as he settled on one of the wooden benches that ran the length of the locker bay. Resting the clipboard on his thighs, he placed the tip of the pen where Anthony had indicated. After another calming breath, Pierce painstakingly wrote his name.

He took another few minutes to work out most of the words on the form. As much as he trusted Anthony, he didn't want to be too dependent on him. After confirming where he needed to be and when, he handed the pen and board back to Anthony.

"Thanks, Anth." Pierce stood and grabbed his clean clothes from his locker. "I think I'm gonna go for a run."

Anthony's snort drew Pierce's attention to his friend's grinning face. "You just showered, and you're gonna go work out some more?"

Pierce shrugged.

"You could have just run on the treadmill," Anthony

pointed out, using a thumb to point over his shoulder.

"Naw," Pierce told him. "Not that kind of run." Grinning, he pulled his jeans on underneath his towel. Then he dropped the damp fabric as he zipped and buttoned. "Ready to get out in nature and get some fresh air."

After another nod, Anthony turned and waved the clipboard. "Have fun."

Pierce grunted in acknowledgment as he pulled his gray wife-beater over his head. After pulling on his socks and shoes, he picked up his bag and headed out of the gym. Feeling the warm sun's rays on his cheeks coupled with the cool spring breeze, he grinned.

Yeah. Nature it is.

Opening his soft-top's door, Pierce climbed into his *Jeep*. He tossed his bag into the back and shut the door. Firing up the engine, he headed north.

Even though Pierce had just worked his arms on the bag, he still felt energized. He always seemed to have an excess of energy. The physical activity acted as a release for that, otherwise he would never get any sleep. He'd struggled with that as a kid, since school forced him to sit in a chair and listen to a teacher drone on and on for hours at a time — then the time spent doing homework.

Dismissing a past he had no ability to change, Pierce turned his *Jeep* onto a county road leading into the hills. He thought it was a little ironic that he'd ended up a receptionist for the town's police station. Sheriff Stillwell was understanding however, and he had bought Pierce a desk that he could raise and lower, allowing him to stand while doing his work.

The sheriff didn't even mind that Pierce danced while working. The man smiled or chuckled occasionally, but the noise was never malicious. He said as long as the work was done correctly, Pierce could do it however he wanted.

Finding the little-used trailhead he wanted, Pierce turned onto it. He parked, noticing a number of motorcycles in the lot. Peering over them, he wondered what it would feel like to ride on one. Pierce had a soft-top *Jeep* with roll-bars, and he figured it would feel similar to when he removed the canvas.

With that thought, another bounced through Pierce's mind. It was almost warm enough to do just that.

Maybe when I get home.

Oh, I should check the forecast, first.

After slipping from his vehicle, Pierce reached in and grabbed a light jacket from the back. He tied the arms around his waist, then shut the door. Since it was a little cooler in the hills, he wanted it just in case.

"Oh. And water and a couple of granola bars," Pierce reminded himself. He rounded his vehicle and opened the passenger door. After snagging a satchel from the floorboard, he grabbed the granola bars from the glove box and a couple bottles of water from the case of them he kept in the back. "And we're ready."

Pierce figured a shrink would have a field day with the fact that he talked to himself, but he didn't give a shit.

Heading up the trail, Pierce swung his arms, stretching his shoulders, biceps, and triceps as he started his hike. He hadn't gone far when he realized he heard voices. Figuring it was the guys who had been on the motorcycles, Pierce glanced around with interest.

When Pierce rounded the next bend, he noticed a flash of yellow between two trees to his right. He paused and squinted, peering into the gloom. It took him a second, but he realized someone was over there.

Pierce glanced at the trail, nibbling his bottom lip. The rules of hiking were to stay on the trail, but he knew a lot of people had picnics, too. Just as he turned, deciding it was none of his business, Pierce saw a face between the branches . . . and it was someone he knew.

"Deputy Anderson," Pierce murmured, heading in that direction. The man, Marrakesh Anderson — Mac to his friends —

had recently retired when he'd found the love of his life in a cute twinky guy named Deter. Pierce had thought they'd left the area.

Is that really him?

Lifting a branch, Pierce eased through a break in the trees. "Hey, Deputy Anderson," he called, grinning at the man. When the guy turned, Pierce lifted his hand in greeting as he moved into the clearing. "Hi, there! I didn't know you were back in town."

Deputy Anderson's eyes widened, and his lips parted, his surprise etched over his features. "Pierce." He darted his gaze around the area as he strode toward him. "Hey, man. How are you?"

Pierce opened his mouth to answer, but an odd popping and cracking sound drew his attention. Focusing left, he gaped as he stumbled backward a step. There . . . right before his eyes . . . was the oddest damn thing he'd ever seen.

"Th-There was a zebra . . . and now he's a man!"

Lifting his hands in placation, Deputy Anderson stepped before him, blocking his view of the naked, blushing male. "Pierce, just calm down. Take a breath." He rested his hands on Pierce's shoulders and squeezed lightly. "I can explain."

Staring at his ex-co-worker, Pierce cried, "How the hell can you explain *that*?"

Chapter Two

"Well, this is awkward," Daevon Ferdmin commented mildly as he watched Mac try to soothe a huge, clearly shocked human. Lifting a brow, he turned his attention to Diego, who was holding a blushing Zachary. "Does this kind of thing happen often?"

Daevon didn't know the group well. He'd only arrived in town less than a week before. The group of shifters were waiting for their alpha—as well as the rest of their pack—to return from an emergency trip overseas.

Waiting for Alpha Kontra and the others to arrive, Daevon had agreed to go running with the remaining shifters in the pack.

"No," Diego replied as he rubbed his hand up and down Zachary's back. Dipping his head, he whispered, "Grab your jeans and stop worrying about this. Mac will handle his friend."

Turning his attention back toward the big human, Daevon dismissed Zach's naked limping form as he went to retrieve his clothes. Diego followed him. Daevon bet the wolf shifter would help his zebra shifter mate dress in record time.

Instead, Daevon admired the handsome human who'd interrupted their outing. He stood a good half-foot taller than his own five-foot-nine stature, and with his hair shorn so close to his skull, Daevon wasn't entirely certain how dark a blond it was. The man—Pierce, according to Mac—had wide shoulders, brawny arms and legs, and an eight-pack on display under his gray wife-beater t-shirt.

Damn. What a fine specimen of maleness.

Surprise filled him when that thought went through him. Daevon wasn't usually attracted to hulking men. Instead, he enjoyed dalliances with males around his own size.

Interest pooling in his gut, Daevon drew closer to the human. As soon as Pierce's musky aroma wafted across his senses, his mouth began to water. His wolverine growled in his mind, urging him to get closer to him.

Holy Christ on a cracker! Pierce is my mate!

Grinning widely, Daevon tuned in to what Mac was telling Pierce.

"Let me introduce you to a friend of mine," Mac was saying. Moving one hand from his shoulder to beckon to Prudhoe, he added, "He's much better at explaining these things than I am."

For a second, Daevon wondered why Mac would draw Prudhoe's attention. The man was a fae warrior. He was bonded with the human Korvyn. They had only come on the run to spend time with Korvyn's half-brother. Rusty was a serval cat shifter who was mated to a scorpion shifter.

As Prudhoe reached for Pierce's hand, as if intending to shake, Daevon spotted the slight glow of the fae's lavender eyes. Realization hit. Prudhoe was fae . . . and he could alter memories.

"Stop," Daevon barked, closing the last few steps between himself and the trio. "Don't touch him."

Mac and Prudhoe both turned to face him. Their scents gave away their surprise. "Daevon?" Mac questioned slowly. "It's fine. Prudhoe can handle this."

"I understand how you expect Prudhoe to handle it," Daevon commented, holding up his hand. "But it's Fate's wish that he learn of us."

Prudhoe crossed his arms over his expansive torso. "How do you figure that?" At least the glow of magick had faded from his eyes.

Daevon eased closer to Pierce, who was glancing between them all. His brows were furrowed, and the acrid scent of confusion filled the afternoon air. He'd shoved his hands into his jeans pockets and hunched his shoulders.

Everything about him screamed discomfort. There was even a faint trace of fear perfuming the air.

His shifter instinct drove him to clear that scent damn fast.

"Pierce is my mate," Daevon claimed, reaching out to Pierce. He gently wrapped his hands around Pierce's right forearm. "I'm Daevon Ferdmin." He offered the quiet human an encouraging smile. "Mac here called you Pierce. Pierce what?"

"Uh, Pierce Rinkon."

Daevon led Pierce toward a soft patch of grass at the far edge of the small clearing that all the shifters had been using to strip and change in, and he eased onto his ass. Mac and Rusty—who'd lived in the area for years—had assured them all that the trail was rarely used. Otherwise, they would have gone further up the path, but Korvyn—who was in a wheelchair—hadn't wanted to be a burden.

Of course, with Prudhoe's impressive fae strength, nothing could have been further from the truth.

"Please have a seat, Pierce," Daevon encouraged, tugging the big human down next to him. He stretched his legs out before him, crossing them at the ankles. "So, you've had your first experience in learning that the world is a much bigger place than you thought."

"Bigger place?" Pierce rubbed his large palm over his shortly cropped hair. "What do you mean?"

Mac settled on Pierce's other side, crossing his legs. "What Daevon means is that what you saw was a shifter changing from one form to another." He used his hand to sweep the area. "My friends and I came out here to take on our animal form, so we could go for a run in a secluded area." Patting

Pierce's thigh companionably, Mac told him, "This area is so rarely used, I didn't think anyone would be out and about." Then he chuckled and added, "That and it's pretty hard to see into this clearing unless you're looking for it."

"I heard you talking and saw Deter's yellow shirt," Pierce told him quietly. "I was gonna keep going, but then I saw your face so was gonna say hi." Glancing between them, he asked, "How can the world get bigger? And what's a shifter?"

Before Daevon could answer, Mac jumped in again. "When Daevon says the world is bigger, he doesn't mean in an actual physical sense."

Pierce cocked his head, his confusion evident. "Then what do you mean?" he asked, focusing on him. "I don't get it."

Daevon opened his mouth, then closed it again. "Well—"

"You need to explain in a concise, straightforward manner, Daevon," Mac told him. "Something easy to understand." Then he patted Pierce's thigh again, drawing his attention. "He doesn't mean the world is bigger in a physical way. He means in a mental way." Mac tapped his temple. "You are learning about something new. Something most people don't know, and it is a secret that you'll have to keep for the rest of your life."

Even as Daevon bristled at the simplistic way Mac was speaking to Pierce, his mate nodded, not seeming upset in the least.

"Okay. So . . . shifters then?" Pierce glanced between them. "What is that?"

Mac cleared his throat as he lifted a brow and focused on Daevon. "You want to explain? Or should I?"

"I'll give it a go, and you can fill in anything I miss," Daevon stated, needing Pierce's focus on him. "Sound okay?"

Lifting his hand in a *go ahead* gesture, Mac nodded.

Concise and straightforward.

"In the world, there are more than just humans," Daevon stated as he reached out and took Pierce's hand. While Pierce glanced at where he clasped him in obvious surprise, he didn't comment or attempt to pull away. Taking that as a win, Daevon continued. "There are shifters out there. People who can change from a human form to an animal one and back again."

Pierce's eyes widened, and his lips parted. He sucked in a sharp gasp. After glancing around, he leaned close to Daevon and whispered, "You mean like in those werewolf movies?" A shudder worked through his big body, leaving tension in its wake. "I don't like horror movies. They give me funny dreams."

"No, not like that," Daevon quickly assured, massaging Pierce's hand. "Yes, we can change into an animal, but we are still us when we're that animal. We don't attack people, and we don't bite people and turn them into more shifters."

"We?" Pierce's eyes widened, and he attempted to tug his hand away. "You, too?"

Oops.

"Take a deep breath, Pierce," Mac rumbled as he rubbed Pierce's back soothingly. After Pierce had obeyed and had begun to calm—although he did continue to nibble his bottom lip—Mac told him, "Lots of people you know are shifters, and we've never done anything to hurt you. Have we?"

Pierce gazed at Mac with wide eyes as he slowly shook his head. "A-And that guy wasn't a w-werewolf anyway." His own words appeared to help him calm down, and Pierce licked his lips as he looked around, perhaps searching for Zach, who was no longer in the clearing. "He was a zebra."

"Not a werewolf," Daevon corrected gently. "Just wolf or wolf shifter. And Zach's partner, Diego, does turn into a wolf."

"That was the big, dark-haired guy holding him," Pierce commented, showing that even when freaking out, he was observant. "They're partners?"

"When addressing a human, yes, they call each other partner." Since Pierce seemed to be taking everything in stride, he decided to expand on the knowledge. He needed his mate to understand what he meant to him, after all. "When around paranormals, they refer to each other as mates."

Pierce cocked his head, and his eyes narrowed. "Paranormal? What's that?" Then he turned from Daevon and focused on Mac. "I don't understand."

Mac sighed deeply as he patted Pierce's thigh again. "A paranormal is any sentient being that is not a human."

"Like aliens?" Pierce asked.

Daevon couldn't contain his chuckle. "Not aliens. Those are from outer space."

Pierce gaped at him. "There really *are* aliens?"

Realizing they were getting way off track, and confused by the way Pierce kept getting distracted, Daevon scowled. "No. Err . . . not that I know of." He squeezed Pierce's hand. "Focus, handsome. Shifters, remember?"

Swallowing hard enough to cause his Adam's apple to bob, Pierce hunched his shoulders. "Sorry."

Daevon's heart constricted as guilt swamped him. His wolverine snarled in his mind. He grimaced, hating that he'd pulled that response from his mate.

Shit.

Mac glared at Daevon, curling his lip at him.

Concise and straightforward.

Recalling that advice, Daevon realized there was something more going on with Pierce than simple confusion and being overwhelmed by information. "No, I'm sorry," he murmured. Lifting his hand to his mate's jaw, he urged him to lift his chin and meet his gaze. The amount of embarrassment filling not only his eyes but his scent caused the hairs on Daevon's nostrils to burn. "I got us off track. So, answer me this. Do you believe in soul mates?"

Pierce scoffed and rolled his eyes. Although his actions

were answer enough, he still stated, "Naw. That's not a real thing."

"It is real to shifters. We simply call our soul mate a mate." Daevon flicked his gaze to Mac, hoping for guidance, but the man just shrugged, then nodded. "That person, our mate, whether they be a man, woman, human, or some other species of paranormal . . . we bond with that person. We share our lives with them."

Pierce chuckled softly, easing back onto his elbows and staring up, glancing between them. "So, you guys turn into animals, but you can still think and reason while in that form." He bobbed his head. "Okay. That's cool. I won't tell." Rolling his eyes, Pierce stated, "Hell, people think I'm dumb as it is. If they thought I believed in people that turn into animals, then I'd be labeled crazy, too."

Daevon growled low in his throat. "You are not dumb."

Then how the big human spoke and acted ticked off something in his mind.

Was he?

Chapter Three

Sitting on his sofa holding a beer, Pierce stared at the TV screen. He couldn't have said what was on, though. His mind reeled with all the information he'd learned that afternoon.

Wow! Shifters and other creatures that Hollywood bases monster movies on are real.

Except, they aren't monsters.

Pierce could hardly believe that he'd been working right alongside one for years. When Mac—Marrakesh had invited him to call him that, which was nice—had stripped down, he'd done his best not to ogle. The man was pretty fine, after all, and Pierce had never seen him naked.

Of course, all thought of arousal had flown right out of his head—and his body—when Pierce had watched Mac shift.

A Darwin fox. Crazy!

Shaking his head absently, Pierce had to acknowledge that wasn't even the craziest part of it all. The guy who'd stopped Prudhoe from touching him—Daevon Ferdmin—had claimed they were soul mates.

Soul mates? How can I be a soul mate to a smart guy who turns into a wolverine?

That had been sort of scary to see.

Once again, Pierce had struggled to control his reactions. That time, however, it hadn't worked. Seeing Daevon's naked body had caused an instant boner. He'd wanted to crawl over and suck Daevon's half-hard prick to full mast and drink his seed.

What would he taste like?

Pierce hadn't gotten the chance, which was probably a good thing. Daevon's body had shrunk. The sounds of pops and cracks had filled the air, making Pierce cringe. When the wolverine's sharp teeth and claws had formed, it had taken every bit of Pierce's self-control not to crab-walk away from it.

Mac's reassuring hand on his shoulder had helped.

Then Daevon had changed back. They'd chatted, the handsome man sharing a little about himself. He'd told how for the last twenty-two years he'd been a college professor. He'd just retired and, through the Shifter Council, had heard about Kontra Belikov's nomadic biker gang.

Daevon had arrived in town just shy of a week prior, only to learn that Alpha Kontra was away. He was waiting for him to get back. Then Daevon had asked if Pierce had ever thought about traveling.

Pierce had admitted that he had, but he didn't have money for that.

Then Daevon had professed one more whopper.

"I'm almost two-hundred-fifty years old, Pierce," Daevon had claimed. "I've had plenty of time to amass quite a bit of wealth." He'd brought Pierce's hand to his lips and kissed his knuckles. "Anything your heart desires, I would be honored to provide."

Who talks like that?

Daevon and Mac had taken turns explaining how important mates were to a shifter. Then both men had offered to drive him home.

Pierce had declined, needing some time alone. Still, he knew Daevon had followed him on his motorcycle. The shifter had claimed he wanted to make certain Pierce made it home safely.

Does Daevon think I'm too stupid to get here on my own?

After letting out a deep sigh, Pierce took a swig of his beer.

He shook his head, hoping that wasn't it. As he swallowed the brew, he grimaced, realizing it had gone flat.

Huh. I've been sitting here far longer than I thought.

Pierce had never zoned out quite like that before. He finally understood the expression, mind blown. His thoughts circled back to Daevon and how he'd followed him home.

Why?

Maybe I should ask.

Daevon had told him that he would answer anything truthfully. Picking up the remote, he turned off the TV. He grabbed his cell phone and read the time.

Nine-fifty-two.

Pierce hoped it wasn't too late to call even as he pulled up Daevon's number. Hitting the dial button, he lifted the phone to his ear. He listened to the line ring.

"Pierce? Is everything okay?"

The sound of Daevon's warm tenor did funny things to Pierce's insides. Mac had said that was part of the mate-pull. Pierce had never been particularly religious and didn't know how he felt about their belief in gods that manipulated humans.

"Yeah, I'm fine," Pierce immediately replied, swirling his beer in his bottle and watching it slosh. "Got a question."

"Anything."

Pierce scowled at the liquid in the bottle. "How come you followed me home?" Unable to help himself, he demanded, "You think I'm too stupid to find my way?"

"No," Daevon snapped, a growl in his voice. "I don't know who put that idea into your head, but you can get it out right now."

Rolling his eyes, Pierce thought about all the kids at school who'd made fun of him. Bullies were just the first in a long line of people telling him he was dumb or asking if he was stupid or insinuating he was slow — teachers, coaches, tutors, people who were supposed to be his friends. Pierce had accepted he was on the slow side ages ago.

"Look, if you're serious about seeing me for any length of time, you need to accept the facts," Pierce stated with a sigh. He lifted the cool glass bottle to his temple. "I'm slow. That doesn't mean I can't learn or I won't eventually understand something. It just takes me longer." After a second of hesitation, Pierce admitted, "Plenty of people around here know that, and some of them aren't nice about it, but most don't care."

After a few seconds of silence from the line, Daevon murmured, "Okay."

Pierce took a sip of his flat beer, then rested the bottle on his thigh. Tipping his head back on the sofa cushion, he stared at the ceiling. "So, will you answer the question, please?"

"I followed you home because I was worried you were in shock," Daevon told him, his voice quiet. "We had shared so much information with you. When that happens, sometimes it leaves a person dazed." His tone lowered, growing softer. "It can be dangerous to drive like that, and I didn't want anything to happen to you."

All Pierce's uneasiness flowed out of him. He couldn't help but smile. Pierce couldn't remember a time when someone other than his father worried about him.

My father.

"I usually tell my father everything," Pierce commented absently. "Guess this is the first real secret I'll have to keep from him."

"Afraid so, unless he finds a paranormal to mate with."

Pierce nodded, appreciating that Daevon treated him with enough respect to be truthful and straightforward.

"Pierce?"

Right. He can't see me nod.

"I understand," Pierce said around the sudden lump in his throat. "Sorry, I get lost in my head a lot."

"Nothing wrong with that as long as we share everything eventually." Daevon hummed for a second, then asked, "Does your father know you're gay?"

"Oh, yeah." Pierce rolled his eyes as a smirk curved his lips. "Told you I shared everything with him. Told him as soon as I realized it when I was fourteen."

"How'd he take it?"

Pierce furrowed his brows as he recalled the interaction. "I could tell it took him by surprise because I've always been athletic. He asked if I was sure. I told him I was." Sighing, he admitted, "Then he told me it could make my life harder and to be careful who I told. He enrolled me in martial arts classes at the gym, but I really struggled with that. Eventually, I found boxing, and I excelled." Laughing softly, Pierce added, "Dad doesn't understand why I like a sport where people are trying to punch my head in, since I'm already slow, and I try to explain that it's about learning to avoid and block punches as much as landing them. He frowns and nods, but I don't think he really understands."

"What about your mother?"

A low growl of anger burned through Pierce as he thought about the woman who'd bore him. "I don't have a mother."

"Ah, there must be a story there," Daevon murmured.

Pierce guessed Daevon wanted to hear it, too, but he didn't feel up to sharing it. "What about you?" he asked instead. "What about your family? Are you close to anyone?"

"I lost my parents when a rival pack attacked them for their territory over a century ago." Daevon's voice took on a note of sadness, but it almost instantly cleared as he kept talking. "I do have a brother that I speak with regularly. Deacon. He's a badger shifter, though. Not a wolverine. He's gonna meet up with me in a few months, wherever we are."

Confusion filled Pierce... for a couple of reasons. "Badger? How can you be brothers if you're different kinds of shifters?"

"My mother was a badger shifter. My father, a wolverine." Daevon snorted softly. "When Fate paired them, it created quite a stir in my father's wolverine pack. They kicked him out, but my mother's badger clan welcomed them with open arms."

"Bigots come in all forms," Pierce commented absently before swigging the last of his beer. He rose to his feet and headed to the kitchen to get another.

"That there is," Daevon confirmed. "Anyway, a shifter born of mixed breeding like that can take after either the mother or father, and the parents don't know until they shift for the first time."

"Can you guys shift from birth?" After grabbing the beer, Pierce returned to the sofa, feeling more relaxed now that they weren't talking about him.

"No, many breeds start shifting a few years before puberty," Daevon told him. "There are a few aquatic shifter species that are born in their animal form, like seahorses, but they're extremely rare." Scoffing, he told Pierce, "I can only guess at how freaked out that shifter would be the first time they became human."

Pierce nodded absently, trying to imagine that. He couldn't, so instead, he changed the subject again. "So, you claim I'm your mate, but you're really smart." He heaved a sigh, pausing before voicing his fears.

"You are my mate, Pierce," Daevon inserted. "A shifter recognizes his mate by scent. I knew you immediately." Then a low, hungry-sounding growl came through the line. "And I look forward to the day you allow me to claim you."

A tingle traveled down Pierce's spine, causing the hairs on his nape to stand on end. His gut tightened, and his blood flowed to his prick. Reaching down, he adjusted himself, grunting upon feeling the stimulation.

"Damn," Pierce grumbled. "Never gotten hard from someone's voice before."

Daevon's husky chuckle came through the line, causing Pierce's prick to twitch. "Like the sound of my voice, do you?"

Pierce moaned softly, knowing Daevon had deepened his voice on purpose. *Or maybe he's aroused, too.* "Yeah," Pierce answered honestly, unbuttoning and unzipping his jeans. As he lifted his hips and pushed his pants down to his ankles, freeing his erection, he grunted. "Do you like the sound of my voice?" he managed to ask as he grabbed his dick.

"Oh, very much," Daevon quickly told him. "I'm sitting in my hotel room hard as a rock from our chat."

Letting out a shuddering breath, Pierce slowly teased his fingertips up and down his length. He spread his legs a little, offering his swollen balls more room. Sighing deeply, he rested his head against the couch cushion and brought that image up in his mind's eye.

"You're a handsome guy when you're naked." Pierce wondered what Daevon's cock looked like hard and weeping. "If I asked you to come over here so I could fuck you, would you?"

"In a heartbeat, Pierce," Daevon replied, desire filling his voice. "But you need to remember what that means to me, as your mate."

Right. That.

Sighing again, Pierce gripped his balls and tugged a little, trying to ease his need. He shouldn't be thinking with his dick. This was serious shit to the shifter.

"I've never been in a relationship, Daevon," Pierce told him, knowing he needed to be honest. "Never met anyone who I wanted to stay with, and never met anyone who wanted to deal with my shit every day." Knowing he needed to share his concerns, Pierce quickly added, "You taught college classes. Won't you get bored with some dumb jock like me?"

All my other fuck buddies eventually did . . . even Anthony, although that could be more due to him being so deep in the closet.

Chapter Four

Daevon bit back a low growl. Arousal thrummed through his body, mixing with the indignant rage at the way someone—or more like plenty of someones—had made Pierce feel. One way or another, Daevon vowed to make his mate see that he would love and care for the man unconditionally.

I'm just not certain how to do that.

First—"Pierce, I could never get bored with you." Knowing talk was cheap, Daevon continued, "I admit, I don't know how Fate chooses a match, and I know that we will have to work at our relationship. No relationship is roses and sunshine all the time." Daevon paused, trying to decide where he was going with his statement. *Right.* "But I have never seen a fated pair not work out when both are committed to working at it."

Pierce remained quiet for a moment. Daevon would have thought he'd lost the call, but he could hear his human's deep breaths coming through the line. He tried to be patient, but it was difficult.

As a tenured college professor, Daevon had had control of everything from his schedule to his class assignments. Now that he'd retired and he was waiting for Alpha Kontra, decisions he ruled over were in short supply. Fate sure had a funny way of choosing when to heap on another change.

And maybe that's why she chose now . . . or perhaps Pierce is ready for change, so I was sent to him.

Hmmm.

"How do people work at a relationship?"

Hearing Pierce's quiet question drew Daevon out of his confusing thoughts. There wasn't much of a point in contemplating the motives of the gods. He had no way of confirming his suspicions, so it was a waste of time.

"Well—" Daevon hesitated. It wasn't as though he had a whole hell of a lot of experience in that arena. With that thought in mind, Daevon recalled when Deter and Mac had had a disagreement... or when Prudhoe and Korvyn had been of two minds. "Talking," Daevon blurted out, thinking he'd been quiet too long. "Just like we're doing now. We share our thoughts, our worries. Share our likes and dislikes." Realizing they hadn't done that yet, Daevon added, "For example, you mentioned asking me to come over so you could fuck me. I'm a switch, so I would enjoy that very much. At some point, however, I would not only need to top you to complete our bond, but I would love giving your beautiful body as much bliss as I can manage over and over again."

"Fuck!" Pierce whined, surprising Daevon with how deep and husky he sounded. "Just keep talking about us fucking, and I'll get my rocks off in no time."

"Hell yeah," Daevon whispered, pleased beyond reason that his mate enjoyed his voice and words so much. "Do you have your dick out, Pierce?"

Daevon closed his eyes as he sprawled across the comforter in his hotel room. Pushing aside the towel he'd wrapped around his hips after the shower he'd taken when he'd arrived there—he'd been in desperate need of rubbing one out—he revealed his hard cock. Grabbing his aching rod, Daevon sucked in a harsh gasp.

"Y-Yeah. Yeah, I got my jeans around my ankles, and I'm stroking my hard cock." Pierce groaned, the deep sound causing goose bumps to rise on Daevon's arm. "God, it feels so damn good. Would be better if it was your mouth."

Swallowing the sudden surge of saliva, Daevon moaned. "Gods, if I was there, I would deep-throat your dick over and over." He licked his lips and swallowed again as he imagined it. "Are you short and fat, my mate? Or long and slender?" His gut clenched as he relished the feel of his fingers sliding over his shaft while trying to picture a naked Pierce and his dick. "Tell me."

Pierce's loud groan sounded through the line. Then he said on panting breaths, "L-Long and thick." After hissing, he mumbled, "Circumcised. Sensitive balls. Oh!"

"Are you cupping your balls?" Daevon asked, guessing at what had drawn that throaty *oh* from Pierce's throat. "You pretending it's me rolling your big orbs over my fingers?"

"Yes!" Pierce cried. "So good!"

Daevon's nipples beaded as he listened to Pierce's grunts and moans coming through the line. Grinning, he urged, "That's the way, Pierce. Now squeeze them lightly and tug." As Daevon spoke, he did the same to his own sack, causing his gut to clench. "Are your nipples hard, my mate?" he crooned. "Would you like me to suck and nip at them? Are they sensitive?"

Pierce hissed. "Yessss. That would feel so nice. You'd have to suck hard. Otherwise, I won't feel it," he revealed, sharing how he enjoyed being pleasured. "Would rather have you suck on my balls while you finger my ass."

Groaning, Daevon imagined that. His rush of pleasure at learning that not only did Pierce bottom, but that he seemed to be looking forward to it, caused a zing to shoot down his spine. His testicles tightened, and he knew his orgasm was so damn close.

"Oh, Pierce," Daevon rumbled, releasing his balls so he could jack his dick once more. "I will push my face between your thighs and lick your sack. I'll scrape my fingernail over the sensitive skin of your crack and massage over your hole.

Are you sensitive there? Do you like that?" Hearing Pierce's whines and whimpers through the line enflamed his blood better than his hand on his shaft. "What if I bury my nose in your crack and slide my tongue all over your hole. I'll push into your body and massage the inner muscles of your entrance." Hearing Pierce's groans and grunts increase in volume, Daevon felt his own balls pull tight. "Gods, mate," he cried. "I wanna eat your ass so bad I can practically taste it. Imagining it is making me come."

When Pierce howled through the line, he no longer held back. Daevon cried out his pleasure as his balls unloaded, spurting shot after shot of cum up and out of his throbbing erection. Panting softly, Daevon floated pleasantly on the endorphins surging through his system as well as the knowledge that, in a way, he'd pleased his mate.

"Damn, Daevon," Pierce mumbled after a few minutes. "That was . . ." His voice trailed off on a sigh. "Better than most of the sex I've enjoyed over the years."

Daevon swallowed back his growl. Even as his wolverine snarled possessively in his mind, he reminded himself that Pierce probably hadn't meant to compare their time together with others. People often blurted out random shit when their minds were blissed out on endorphins, and Pierce was blunter than most.

"And it will only get better," Daevon chose to say instead. "When I finally do the things I described, I will ruin you for everyone." Unable to withhold all his possessive tendencies, he grumbled, "My mate to pleasure for eternity."

Pierce cleared his throat before replying, "Eternity is a long time."

Chuckling quietly, Daevon told him, "Some people believe that bonded mates come back in close proximity to each other. That way they can find each other again in their next life."

"Next life?" Pierce snorted. "Are you talking about reincarnation or some shit like that?"

Daevon nodded as he used part of his towel to clean up the sprays of semen covering his chest and groin. Then, remembering Pierce couldn't see that through the line, he snickered at himself. "Some people believe in it."

"Do you?"

The curiosity in Pierce's voice gave Daevon pause. He hummed. "You know. I haven't ever really given it much thought," Daevon admitted. "It's a romantic notion, though."

Deciding a subject change was in order, Daevon asked, "Are you available tomorrow, Pierce? I'd like to see you."

Pierce grunted, and Daevon heard the sound of fabric cushions shifting. Then there was the rustling of clothing. Finally, Pierce sighed before replying.

"Sorry. Had to get my shirt off. My cum was drying and starting to itch. What was that?"

Daevon smirked, finding that he enjoyed Pierce's openness. "Can I meet you for lunch tomorrow?"

"Uh . . . yeah. Where?"

Pulling up a mental map of the town, Daevon thought about the restaurants he'd tried over the last few days. He offered a couple of options, then asked, "Unless you have a favorite you'd prefer?"

"Oh, I like O'Reilly's," Pierce told him. "Their burgers and onion rings are fantastic."

"All right. There then." Daevon grinned, anticipation filling him upon confirming that he would soon see his mate again. "Eleven-thirty work for you?"

"Yeah."

As loath as Daevon was to lose the connection to Pierce, he knew it was time to say good-bye. "I'll see you tomorrow, Pierce," he murmured. Then he couldn't help but add, "I look forward to seeing you again."

"You know . . . me too." Pierce's voice actually sounded a bit surprised but also pleased. "Night, man."

"Goodnight."

Daevon pulled his phone from his ear and saw the line had been disconnected. Heaving himself to his feet, he placed his phone on the nightstand and plugged it into the charger. He tossed the soiled towel into the corner, then shoved the comforter and sheet down.

Crawling into bed, Daevon grabbed a pillow and clutched it close. He closed his eyes and dreamed of when he would be holding his mate instead.

Daevon arrived at O'Reilly's fifteen minutes early. He just couldn't sit around his hotel room anymore. With anticipation thrumming through him, he entered the pub-style restaurant and smiled at the hostess.

"Hello again, Daevon," Cathy greeted, picking up a menu as she beamed a smile at him. "Can't get enough of our shepherd's pie, huh?" With a wink, she added, "Told you it was fantastic."

Grinning, Daevon nodded. He'd been there just the prior day for lunch, and he'd taken Cathy's recommendation to try the lamb dish. It had indeed been fantastic.

Pointing at the single menu Cathy carried, Daevon told her, "Actually, I'm meeting someone today, so there will be two of us."

"Oh, yeah?" Cathy turned back to the stand and grabbed another menu. Smiling at Daevon again, she asked, "Who ya meetin'?"

Daevon wasn't surprised at Cathy's nosiness. She'd flirted with him each time he came in. The first time Daevon had been in, she'd brazenly asked if his wife would be joining him later.

"No, I don't have a husband," Daevon had casually replied.

Cathy had laughed as she nodded. "Gotcha." That didn't stop her from flirting, though.

"I'm meeting Pierce Rinkon." Daevon didn't see a reason not to be truthful, since she would see them together soon enough. Plus, then she could point Pierce toward him. "Do you know him?"

Grinning over her shoulder as she led him toward a booth, Cathy nodded. "Yup." She placed a menu on each side. "Not meeting up for intellectual conversation, I hope." Stepping back, Cathy continued to smile as she blithely maligned Daevon's mate. "Because you sure won't get it there. Are you asking him to teach you boxing or something?"

Daevon clenched his jaw against the desire to snap at her. After a calming breath, he eased onto the bench seat that faced toward the door, so he could watch for Pierce. Then he offered Cathy a cool smile.

"I'm meeting him for a date."

Cathy's jaw sagged open. Her cheeks took on a pinkish hue. Then she grinned. "Well, at least the scenery will be nice." With a wink, she headed back toward the front desk. Only Daevon's shifter hearing allowed him to make out her mumbled, "Damn, must not want intellectual conversation in the bedroom."

Growling softly, Daevon shook his head. He took several slow deep breaths to calm down.

Is this what my mate has to deal with on a regular basis?

Daevon wondered if he could change that. Then he saw the door open, and his mate walked inside. His heart hammered in his chest as his blood flowed south, causing his dick to plump.

Gods, Pierce is stunning.

Chapter Five

Pierce spotted Daevon sitting in a booth halfway down an aisle to the left and immediately turned in that direction. Unable to help himself, he grinned when he saw the handsome dark-haired man sweep his gaze over him with clear appreciation. As it had been years since Pierce had tried dating, he'd struggled with what to wear.

It seemed that his faded, form-fitting jeans and light-blue polo shirt met with Daevon's approval.

"Snagged the professor's attention, huh, Pierce?" Cathy commented as Pierce headed past her station. "How'd you manage that, ya lucky dog?"

Pierce shrugged as he greeted Cathy. "Not sure how that happened." Then, remembering an expression he'd heard, he offered, "Opposites attract?"

Cathy snickered as she smirked at him. "Got that right."

Having nothing else to contribute, Pierce turned his attention to Daevon. He saw the way his brows were furrowed as he glanced between them and wondered if something was wrong. Pierce preferred the appreciative expression better.

"Hi, Daevon," Pierce greeted upon reaching the table. He slid into the bench seat opposite the shifter and smiled at him. "Sorry I'm late. I hope you weren't waiting long."

"Hi, Pierce." Daevon reached across the table and rested his fingertips on Pierce's hand. "You're not late. I was so eager to see you, I ended up here early."

Pierce grinned broadly, and an odd flutter erupted in his belly.

Huh.

Turning his hand over, Pierce threaded his fingers with Daevon's.

Maybe this dating thing won't be so hard.

"Oh my god," a dark voice grumbled. "The least you faggots could do is keep that shit outa public places."

Or not.

Pierce yanked his hand away and grabbed his menu. His cheeks flamed, and he stared at the table. He desperately wished the server had arrived with their waters because his mouth had just gone dry.

"Isn't it odd that some people feel using vile language in public is acceptable, but they take issue with two men holding hands?"

Daevon's chilly tone drew Pierce's attention back to him. Seeing the man staring to his right, he followed Daevon's gaze. Pierce felt his eyes widen upon seeing Bill and Stan seated at a square table nearby. A pair of women accompanied them.

"Are you talkin' ta me, fag?" Bill asked with a sneer.

Daevon smirked at him. "Just commenting on the poor language choices of certain people in the room." Rolling one shoulder, he added, "If you take exception to that, perhaps you have a guilty conscience."

"I ain't guity o' nothin'," Bill snapped.

"Other than butchering the English language, of course," Daevon responded glibly. Then he turned his focus on Pierce and leaned forward. "Did you know that *ain't* isn't really a word? It's slang, betraying bad language habits."

Pierce's lips parted as he stared at Daevon in shock. He had never seen anyone intentionally intimidate Bill before. The man was six-foot-one and sported a heavily muscled build. His belligerent attitude also contributed to people giving him a wide berth.

Realizing Daevon had asked him a question, Pierce shook

his head. "No. I didn't know that."

"Also, because the word ain't is used in place of isn't, which indicates a negative, then he used the word nothing, which is also a negative, they cancel each other out." Daevon waggled his brows as he finished, "The meaning of what the man said is actually, *I am guilty of something*." He grinned as he reached across the table and stroked his fingertips along Pierce's knuckles. "Isn't the English language fascinating?"

Pierce nodded on instinct. "Yeah." Although, in truth, he didn't really understand everything Daevon had just said.

"Why you piece of ass-licking shit!" Bill shouted as he jumped to his feet.

Tensing, Pierce prepared to rise, intending to defend his much-smaller lunch companion.

"Is there an issue here, sir?" a young woman asked. She carried a couple of glasses of water and set them before Pierce and Daevon. Focusing on them, she smiled, "My apologies it took me so long to get these over here. I'm Wendy, and I'll be your server today."

"Yeah, there's an issue here," Bill cut in, stepping up to their table. He pointed at them. "Them there is faggots, and I don't want them seated near me."

"Odd, you don't seem to have an issue with smacking my ass in the gym locker room," Pierce blurted out. Then he felt his face heat even more. He couldn't remember the last time he'd blushed so badly and figured he looked like a ripe tomato.

"What did you just say about me?" Bill snarled, lifting his hand in a fist.

"Sir, this restaurant doesn't discriminate against sexual orientation," Wendy stated. While her cheeks were a pinkish hue, betraying her unease, she stood tall and sported a serious expression. "If you would like me to move you to another table, I can, but if you continue to harass other customers, I'm going to have to ask you to leave."

Bill gaped as Stan rose and stood next to him. "Are you saying you would make us move because of a pair of cocksuckers?" Stan asked, his face darkening.

"I offered you the opportunity to move, since you don't care for your current seating," Wendy countered, focusing on Stan. "And this is a family pub. Please don't use that sort of language here."

"Bill, please," the blonde woman who'd been sitting to his left called. "Please sit down. Let's just finish our meal and go."

Curling his lip, Bill crossed his arms over his chest and scowled at Wendy. "Bring our check and some boxes. We're leaving."

"Of course," Wendy replied briskly.

She didn't get the chance, however. Cathy arrived right then with the requested boxes in one hand and a billfold in the other. "Here is your ticket, sir." Cathy placed the boxes on the table. "Would you like me to package your leftovers?"

"We'll get it," the dark-haired woman replied softly, reaching for the box.

"Here," Bill grumbled, pulling a card from his wallet and placing it in the billfold without looking at it. He held it out to Wendy.

Taking it, Wendy told them, "I'll be right back, sir." She turned her attention to Daevon and Pierce. "I'm sorry for the delay. I'll be right back to get your drink orders."

"It's no problem at all," Daevon assured, smiling at her. "Not your fault, but will you put in an order of your chili cheese fries, please?"

Wendy returned Daevon's smile with a bright one of her own. "Of course."

As soon as Cathy and Wendy went their separate ways, Bill rested his hands on their table. He glared at Daevon and hissed in a low voice, "Watch your back, little cocksucker."

With a Gentle Nudge

He sneered, "I can't wait to catch you alone."

"It would be the hubris of a jock to underestimate a small man," Daevon replied, relaxing on his seat and smiling coolly at Bill.

Bill's eyebrows furrowed, but he didn't respond. Instead, he turned his attention on Pierce. "And I can't wait until Saturday. I'm gonna bust you up."

Pierce had no idea how to respond. Fortunately, Wendy returned with his ticket.

Straightening, Bill took the folder and returned to his table. Pierce wasn't the only one who kept an eye on the group as they left the restaurant.

Daevon chuckled. "Well, that was interesting." Smiling at Pierce, he asked, "Is every date with you going to turn into an adventure?"

"I-I don't—" Pierce grabbed his water and took a deep swallow. "Sorry about that."

"No need to apologize," Daevon countered, once again teasing his fingertips across Pierce's knuckles. "There are jerks like that everywhere." Then his eyes narrowed. "However, I get the feeling you know him well, and what's going on on Saturday?"

Before Pierce could reply, Wendy stood before them. "Hello again, gentlemen." While her cheeks were still tinged with pink, telling him she was probably still flustered, she smiled brightly at them. "I imagine you haven't had time to decide on a meal, but do you know what you'd like to drink?"

"I'll take an iced tea," Pierce told her, even though he would have preferred a beer.

Daevon never pulled his focus from Pierce as he told her, "A raspberry lemonade, please."

"I'll have those out in a minute." Then Wendy headed away.

"So, what are you getting?"

Pierce glanced from the menu to Daevon and back again. "Uh, I usually just get the burger and onion rings, like I mentioned yesterday." Grimacing, he mumbled, "It's easier than trying to read the menu."

Daevon cocked his head. "You have trouble reading?"

Nodding, Pierce admitted, "I have really bad dyslexia. I *can* read, it's just . . . I'm slow, and it's tough." He shrugged. "It's easier to get what I know."

"Well, if you want to try something else, I'd be happy to read the menu to you." Daevon winked as he lowered his voice to a husky rumble. "It would give me an excuse to sit next to you instead of across from you."

Pierce felt his blood heat, and he shifted restlessly in his seat as his prick thickened. "You're not shy. Are you?" Rubbing the back of his neck, he admitted, "Holding hands just might be my limit right now."

Daevon's brows lifted. "Oh. I'm not thrusting you out of the closet, am I?" He straightened, easing his hands away from Pierce as he picked up his menu.

Shaking his head, Pierce smiled. "Naw. I don't advertise it by wearing pink or yellow, but I'm not in the closet." He shrugged. "Everyone at work knows, and if anyone asks, I'm honest. Most people just don't ask and assume I'm straight." Grinning, Pierce waved his hand at himself. "Not surprising, really."

"Okay. Good." Daevon then peered at the menu. "So, how do you know the asshole?"

"That's Bill. He goes to the same gym as me." Pierce lifted his water and took a swig. Setting it back on the table, he remembered Daevon's earlier question. "And we're both in a boxing match on Saturday, so I may end up facing him." Frowning, Pierce admitted, "He's just as big an asshole in the ring as he is in real life. Tries to get away with certain cheap shots. He's been disqualified a time or two, but he still keeps trying it."

Daevon's brows furrowed into a scowl, and his eyes narrowed. Lines of tension appeared on his neck, and he clenched his hands. His knuckles whitened.

"You are—" With the appearance of Wendy, Daevon snapped his mouth shut. Instantly, he cleared his expression and relaxed his hands. Daevon smiled at their waitress.

"Here are your drinks, gentlemen," Wendy said, placing one in front of each of them. "And your chili cheese fries." After adding the huge platter of thick, steak-cut fries drenched in chili and cheese in the middle of the table, Wendy added two small plates and two rolls of fabric-napkin-covered silverware. Straightening, Wendy placed the serving tray under her arm and pulled out her order pad again. "So, are you ready? Or have any questions about anything?"

"I'm ready," Daevon confirmed. "What about you, Pierce?"

Pierce nodded and smiled at Wendy. "I'd like your loaded guacamole burger with everything." He knew that meant it would come with cheese, bacon, onions, tomatoes, and pickles. "As the side, how about some onion rings."

Wendy nodded, jotting notes onto her pad. Then she turned and smiled at Daevon.

"I'll take the shepherd's pie," Daevon told her. "Please add a side order of onion rings for me, too."

Grinning while writing, Wendy teased, "Good idea." She lifted her pen from her paper and glanced between them before winking. "Especially if there's gonna be any neckin' between you two later." Then Wendy giggled a little as she headed away.

Pierce cocked his head, confusion filling him. "What did she mean?" His cheeks heated a little as he thought of her words, and he cleared his throat. "Are we gonna be neckin' later?"

Daevon grinned widely as he waggled his brows. "I certainly hope so." Then he stabbed a fry with his fork and scooped it through chili and cheese. "And she was referring to the fact that we are here on a date, and there are certain foods you avoid eating while on a date." Then Daevon met his gaze, and before popping the fry into his mouth, he added, "Unless you both eat them."

"Really?" Pierce picked up his fork and followed Daevon's example, stabbing a fry. "Why is that?"

Date rules? Weird.

"Mmm-hmm," Daevon confirmed as he chewed and swallowed the tasty, greasy goodness. "That way if you kiss" — he winked, then finished — "you both taste similar."

"So onions are to be avoided," Pierce mused. "What else?"

Daevon grinned. "Garlic."

Pierce barked a laugh.

Okay. That makes sense.

Chapter Six

Daevon mentally thanked Wendy for her timely interruption. Hearing that Pierce was going to get into a boxing ring had sent protective anger coursing through him. He'd wanted to demand that his human quit immediately.

He'd almost done it, too. Their waitress arriving with their food had given him time to calm down . . . and to pull his head out of his ass.

No way can I start making demands already.

To Daevon's relief, Pierce seemed to have missed his momentary lapse. Plus, Wendy's comment about the onion rings had given them a new subject to focus on. The way Pierce had commented made it abundantly clear that his mate had been telling the truth the prior evening on the phone.

My mate has never — or rarely — dated.

Controlling his instinct to keep his mate safe at all costs wouldn't be easy, but Daevon knew he needed to do it. He focused on the delicious food and on how happy Pierce seemed to be while eating it. With his need to see his mate happy and provided for easing his concerns, Daevon returned to their prior conversation.

"Last night on the phone, you said you started boxing when you were young," Daevon commented while stabbing another fry. "How often do you compete?"

"Not very often," Pierce admitted. Smirking, his fry hovering close to his lips, he stated, "It's more a way to wear me out and keep me fit. Ya know?" He indicated the food with his fry. "Can't eat like this all the time and expect to keep my eight-pack."

After shoving the food into his mouth, Pierce used his free hand to pat his flat belly.

Daevon's mouth watered. "Gods, I'd love to see that."

Pierce chuckled deeply, then winked. "Maybe after we finish our food, we can head back to my place to do a little of that necking we talked about." Then his cheeks darkened to a pleasingly pink hue, and he cleared his throat. "I, uh, don't have much experience with kissing."

That surprised Daevon . . . and pleased his possessive inner wolverine.

"Really?" Daevon narrowed his eyes as he swept his gaze over Pierce's solid, thickly muscled frame. "Somehow, that surprises me."

Pierce shrugged one boulder of a shoulder before saying, "Most of the guys I meet up with are with me for the fucking, so we don't kiss."

Daevon growled softly. "Well, *we* will kiss," he declared, needing to make his intention clear. "And we are not just fucking, Pierce. We are starting a relationship." Upon seeing his mate lift his brows and how he froze with his fry halfway to his lips, Daevon demanded, "Tell me you understand that, Pierce."

For a long moment, Pierce just stared at him.

Waiting impatiently, Daevon bent the fork he was holding. Just as he realized what he'd done, he heard Pierce mutter, "Yeah. I got it."

Sighing with relief, Daevon offered his mate a wan smile. "Oops." He held up his fork. "My bad."

"Damn." Pierce's brows shot up, and he rubbed his palm over his closely shorn scalp. Sweeping his gaze over Daevon's torso, he leaned closer and whispered, "You must be a hell of a lot stronger than you look."

Daevon nodded. After a furtive glance around, he whispered, "Shifters are stronger than humans, and once we bond, you will grow stronger, too." As he bent his fork back to the proper position, Daevon had another thought. He met Pierce's gaze and told him, "It could make boxing a bit . . . unfair and maybe a little dangerous."

Pierce's focus was on swiping the fry through the chili and cheese as he asked, "How do you mean?"

"If you grow stronger, you would have an unfair advantage in a standard fight," Daevon explained. "And since you would be learning your new strength, you could hit someone harder than you'd intended."

His jaw sagging open, Pierce stared at him wide-eyed. It took him a second to gather himself. "Wow. Okay." Scoffing, he grinned. "Good thing I rarely fight, huh? No one will wonder why I quit getting in the ring with others." Then he ate his fry.

Relief flooded Daevon.

Thank the gods. Crisis averted.

"Better win on Saturday, then," Daevon told him with a wink. "Go out on top."

"Or get pestered about making a return just because they want to fight me," Pierce countered.

Daevon nodded. He hadn't considered that.

Wendy approached and placed their food before them.

The conversation stalled as both men focused on their food. Daevon tried a bite of Pierce's burger, which was excellent. Scooping up a forkful of shepherd's pie, Daevon held it out for Pierce to try. When Pierce reached for the fork, he grinned and pulled it away.

"Ah, ah," Daevon teased. "Open up."

Pierce rolled his eyes. Then with his face flaming, he obeyed.

When Daevon slid his fork into Pierce's mouth, another image popped into his head. He moaned. He so desperately wanted to feel his mate's full lips wrapped around his cock instead of his fork.

Daevon heard Pierce's husky chuckle followed by a deep moan.

Groaning, Daevon shook his head. "Tease," he grumbled.

Pierce winked. "It's good," he mumbled around his mouthful. After swallowing, he added, "What meat is that?"

"Lamb."

"Huh. Don't think I've had lamb before." Pierce bobbed his head as he picked up an onion ring, crushed it to make it flat, and finally dipped the end into a tub of fry sauce. "I'll have to get that the next time I'm here."

"And I will try something else," Daevon stated absently, having trouble focusing on anything but Pierce's mouth as he bit into the onion ring. "That way we can experience new foods."

Pierce lifted his left brow as he chewed. "You're looking at me like you wish I was on the menu."

Daevon groaned, shaking his head, trying to clear it. "I am wishing that," he admitted. Seeing the way Pierce beamed at him, clearly pleased, Daevon chuckled and returned to his food. "Eat fast, handsome. Our next discussion needs to be done behind closed doors."

Nodding, Pierce did just that and began eating swiftly. Both men declined dessert, and Daevon grabbed the check before Pierce could. He rubbed his fingers over his human's wrist, massaging his pulse point as he told him, "You can get the next one. Okay?"

Even as Daevon said it, he knew he was going to try to convince Pierce to always allow him to pay. Seeing the way Pierce narrowed his eyes, then nodded slowly, he guessed Pierce might know what he was thinking. Daevon figured he would have to get over his need to always care for his mate.

He is a grown man, after all.

Just as Daevon and Pierce exited the pub, his phone's ring

caught his attention. He pulled the device from his pocket. Upon seeing the name on the display, he grimaced.

"Something wrong?"

"I need to take this," Daevon admitted, meeting his gaze. "It's Mac." While Pierce nodded, he added by way of explanation, "He's supposed to call me and let me know when Kontra is back in town, plus when I can meet with him."

Pierce nodded again, his eyebrows lifting. "Oh, he's the head of the gang, right?" Then his eyes widened. He glanced around quickly while leaning close. "Is he a shifter, too?"

As Daevon nodded and winked, he answered the call and lifted his phone to his ear. "Hey, Mac."

"Hi, Daevon. Hope I'm not interrupting."

Daevon wasn't going to lie to the fox shifter. "Just finished lunch with Pierce. We're standing in the parking lot." Gripping his mate's fingers, Daevon began leading him to his motorcycle. "What can I help you with?"

"Damn, sorry. Guess I should have called last night after all."

"What's going on?" Worry seeped into Daevon as he leaned against his bike. He released Pierce, then watched him round his ride, openly admiring it. "Something wrong?"

"No, no," Mac hurriedly replied. "Just . . . Kontra got in last night, but since you'd met your mate, I thought you'd want a day to connect with Pierce before talking to him."

"I spent some time on the phone with him last night," Daevon revealed, smiling when he saw the way Pierce skimmed his big hands reverently over the side of a fender. "So, yeah. I appreciate the thoughtfulness."

"Well, Kontra has asked to see you." Mac cleared his throat, then added, "Uh, as soon as you're able."

Daevon rolled his eyes even as he nodded. "Right. Code for *get my ass over there*." Most alphas weren't exceptionally patient people. "Where are you? Or where is he, rather?"

"Look, I could tell him that it'll be a couple of hours," Mac offered, his voice tentative.

"No, don't do that," Daevon insisted. "I don't want to piss him off or put you in an awkward position." He knew Mac was a fairly new member of Kontra's pack. "Just tell me where, and I'll be there shortly."

After Mac had given him the address of a picnic area and trailhead where Kontra and the gang were relaxing that afternoon, Daevon disconnected the call and turned his attention to Pierce.

His mate's hands were shoved in his pockets, and his brows were furrowed. "Gotta go, huh?"

"I do." Seeing the look of disappointment on Pierce's face, Daevon quickly asked, "Would you like to come with me?"

"Me?" Pierce's brows shot up as his confusion perfumed the air. "Why?"

Daevon reached out and gripped Pierce's fingers. He kept their hands low. Remembering his mate's reticence at public displays, he attempted to remain discreet.

"You are my mate," Daevon whispered in reply. "I am meeting with the alpha of a nomadic biker gang. I'd planned to ask to go with him." Realizing that idea could have suddenly changed since he'd met his mate, Daevon admitted, "Since we're building a life together, you should meet him, because I'll need you to decide if you want to make a change like going on the road with him."

Pierce gaped, his eyes going wide. "I-I—" He snapped his mouth shut and shook his head.

For several heartbeats, Daevon feared Pierce was denying him. Unease churned in his gut, and he tightened his grip on his phone. When he heard the plastic creak, he managed to gain control of himself.

"Wow," Pierce muttered. "I didn't expect . . . it's just—" He blew out a breath as he rubbed the back of his neck with his free hand. Finally, meeting Daevon's gaze, Pierce stated, "This is all happening so damn fast."

Daevon nodded. "It happens that way with shifters a lot of the time." Stepping closer, he lifted their twined fingers and pressed a kiss to his mate's knuckles. "Then . . . after we speak with him . . . perhaps we'll go back to your place and discuss the options of how we move forward." Unable to resist, Daevon wiggled his eyebrows. "And maybe we'll intersperse it with some necking."

After another long moment, Pierce nodded.

Daevon was far too old to do a fist-pump . . . but he did one in his head.

Chapter Seven

Riding on a motorcycle was just as ball-tingling as Pierce thought it would be. His skin warmed in the sun despite the breeze. His fingers twitched where he gripped the bars to either side of the motorcycle's small back-rest.

Although, whenever Pierce had imagined riding a motorcycle, he had never expected to be the one in the bitch seat. He easily peered over Daevon's shoulder. Feeling the wind on his chin, he appreciated the half-helmet with the face-shield the other man had given him. It protected most of his face from bugs, since he wasn't quite protected by the windshield.

Pierce's heart hammered for another reason, too. He was about to meet the leader of a biker gang. While he knew Mac wouldn't have joined up with anyone disreputable—he was an ex-deputy, after all—Pierce had still heard rumors.

Hell, he heard rumors about gangs in general. Some of them were one-percenters—the guys who made the majority of people who rode motorcycles—the decent ones—look bad. Kontra was part of a gang that had driven off and practically forced one of those gangs to disappear.

Then Kontra's people had taken over the area . . . sort of. From what Pierce had heard, he had bases of operation out of several states. He wondered if that meant he ran guns or something.

God, I hope not.

"I can feel you trembling back there." Daevon reached back and patted Pierce's leg. "Try to relax. I hear Kontra is a good guy. Firm but level-headed."

"So do I," Pierce admitted. Then something else occurred to him. "He's a shifter, right?"

"Yes."

"What kind?" Feeling his face heat with embarrassment at his blunt question, Pierce quickly added, "Is it okay to ask stuff like that?"

"It's fine as long as we're not around humans who don't know about our kind," Daevon told him, flashing a smile over his shoulder before refocusing ahead. "So if there's someone you don't know around, then don't say anything about paranormals within their earshot."

Pierce nodded. "Got it." That made sense.

Daevon patted his leg again. "And he's a grizzly shifter."

"Holy shit!" Pierce squeaked. "I bet that's intimidating."

Nodding, Daevon added, "So I hear." Then he told him, "From what I understand about these guys, they were all misfit shifters kicked out of their packs or prides or whatnot for being gay. They spent decades traveling the country searching for their mates. Apparently, they all found them, too."

"Is that why you wanted to join them? To travel and search for your mate?"

"Yes, Pierce." Daevon reached back and squeezed his knee. "Not only did I need to create a new identity, because I'd lived in one place for long enough that people started noticing that I don't age, but I also wanted to find my special someone." Daevon squeezed his leg again. "I wanted to find you."

Pierce felt an odd pang in his chest as he heard those words. Rubbing at his chest, he realized just how important he was to this man — this shifter. He'd planned to turn his life upside down and travel with strangers to find him.

"Wow," Pierce muttered, uncertain what else to say.

Then Daevon slowed the motorcycle and turned up a narrow, paved lane. They reached a parking lot filled with motorcycles. A large group of men sat at picnic tables, lounged on the grass, or rested against trees, talking in small groups.

They came in all shapes and sizes, and Pierce recognized a few as having been in the clearing where he'd first met Daevon and learned about shifters.

Pierce pegged the big dark-haired guy with odd silver flecks in his hair as Kontra. There was just something about his presence and bearing that screamed *large and in charge*. The man sat at one of the picnic tables. He had a half-eaten sub sandwich in front of him and a bottle of soda. Several others sat with him, including Mac, and he appeared to be listening to him.

Once Daevon parked, Pierce swung off the bike. "That was fun," he murmured, nerves trickling down his spine. "Um . . . are we safe?" Pierce blurted out the question as he took off his helmet. "They don't mind human mates?"

Damn. Should have thought of that before.

"We are safe," Daevon assured, taking the helmet and placing it on the seat beside his own. He squeezed Pierce's hand, assuring, "We are not in any danger from any of these men. Some of these people are human, too. Remember Deter?"

"Right. Right," Pierce murmured, rubbing his hand over the back of his neck. He took in a deep breath, then took Daevon's hand. "So, let's go talk to him, huh?"

Daevon squeezed his hand, then started toward Kontra and the table.

Kontra peered at them, his dark-eyed gaze sweeping over them. It paused on their joined hands. Then his full, goateed lips curved into a small smile as he rose from the table.

"Greetings, Daevon Ferdmin," Kontra stated, holding out his hand across the picnic table. "Mac says good things about you."

"Thank you." Daevon took Kontra's hand, and they shook. Then he glanced Mac's way, smiling at him. "That's nice of you to say, even though you've only known me a week."

Mac chuckled, grinning widely. "Working as a deputy or

other law enforcement over the last half a century, I learned to have a damn good judge of character."

"Wow. Half a century?" Pierce muttered, cocking his head. Realizing he'd drawn everyone's attention, he winced. "Sorry. Didn't mean to interrupt."

"It's fine," Kontra stated, holding out his hand to him. "I hear you're Daevon's mate. Congratulations."

Pierce reached out and gave the big man's hand a shake. While the shifter squeezed, he didn't attempt to overpower or dominate. Instead, it was firm and perfunctory, and then the man released him.

"As you probably guessed, I'm Kontra Belikov. This is my gang." Kontra waved his hand around to indicate the talking, lounging, and laughing men. Then he pointed at a slender man next to him with sandy-brown hair. "This is my mate, Tim Laurent." Next, he indicated a big man with a scar near his left eye. "My beta, Sam Abbott." Finally, Kontra waved at a black-skinned man with dreadlocks. "And my head enforcer, Mutegi."

Daevon dipped his head in a move that looked respectful. "It's nice to meet you all. Thank you for seeing me."

Kontra nodded again. "I admit, I'm surprised you still wanted to meet me." Retaking his seat, he rested his elbows on the table and pointed at Pierce, but he continued to stare at Daevon. "Since you found your mate here, I would have thought you would plan to stay." Then Kontra smirked as he focused on Pierce. "Unless Sheriff Stillwell is about to lose another employee?"

"Uhhh." Pierce frowned, uncertain of how to respond.

Why would the sheriff lose another employee, and why is Kontra looking at me like that?

"We hadn't discussed our future quite that in-depth, yet," Daevon stated, squeezing Pierce's hand. "I thought it best to find out if we would even have an opportunity to ride with your pack before presenting that option to Pierce."

Kontra nodded. "Ah. I see." Then he scented the air and narrowed his eyes. "Plus, you still haven't bonded, yet. Are you having a hard time accepting shifters, Pierce?"

Pierce felt his cheeks heat as discomfort filled him. His stomach twisted, and butterflies took up residence there. Clearing his throat, he swallowed hard.

"Relax, man," a slender male stated, sauntering up to the table. He rested his hip on the end of the table as he grinned cockily at him. Crossing his arms over his chest, he stated, "Don't fight the pull. Trust me, accepting is well worth it." He waggled his eyebrows. "Especially in the sex department. Mind-blowing."

At the mention of sex, Pierce's mind immediately returned to the epic orgasm he'd had the previous evening just from listening to Daevon describe what he wanted to do to him. His blood heated and flowed south, filling his prick. He shifted his feet, trying to find a more comfortable position without blatantly adjusting his untimely erection.

While most of the men around the table responded by rolling their eyes, Kontra lifted a brow. "Something you need, Jared?" His tone held mild amusement.

The man, Jared, shook his head. "Naw. Just giving our new pal a bit of friendly advice." His expression sobered as he added, "I don't want him to put Daevon through the misery I put Carson through."

A tall Native American slipped an arm around Jared's waist and pulled him to his side. "No dwelling on a mistake long forgotten," he told Jared. Rubbing the back of his forefingers along Jared's jaw, he reminded, "Everything worked out in the end."

"I know, Carson," Jared replied, confirming Pierce's guess at who the guy was. He waggled his eyebrows as he cut his attention back to Pierce, his lips curving into a leer. "I'm just offering a fellow human some valuable words of wisdom."

Pierce frowned, cocking his head. "You think I should mate with Daevon because the sex is so great?" Then he focused on his date. "How would he even know it would be great between us?"

Daevon chuckled softly. "I'm sure that's not what he means, and he knows it's great because sex between mates is always far more intense than with anyone else could ever be."

"Huh." Pierce nodded. "Okay." Feeling a sudden possessive need to touch—all that talk about sex made him want to stake a claim—Pierce wrapped his arm around Daevon's shoulders and held him close. "So, are you guys part of Kontra's pack, too?"

Carson shook his head. "No, just traveling with them for a bit while we remake our identities." He held out his hand. "I'm Carson."

"You have to remake your identities?" Pierce asked after shaking his hand. He saw them nod, then remembered how Daevon had said something similar. "Right . . . every couple of decades." Squeezing Daevon's shoulder, he asked, "So, you wanted to meet with Kontra to know if we could travel with him and his guys, uh . . . if I wanted to?"

Daevon rubbed up and down Pierce's spine as he nodded, offering him an encouraging smile. "Whatever you want, my mate. We'll go at your speed." His expression turned pained, "Even if that means you don't want to bond right away."

"But you do want to," Pierce pressed. "That's what you came here for."

"I came here to find the safety of a nomadic pack and, by extension, find my mate." Daevon squeezed his side, hugging him close. "I found you."

Pierce glanced around at everyone. He noticed a number of understanding looks. No one appeared judgmental or even frowned at him.

Would that change when they discovered his faults?

Meeting Daevon's gaze again, Pierce murmured, "I always wanted to travel, but shouldn't you tell them I'm a bit dim first?" He glanced around furtively before meeting Daevon's gaze. "'Cause I can't learn to ride a motorcycle like they do. Will they think it's weird for two guys to ride together all the time? Some people might cause trouble for 'em."

"While I know how to drive a motorcycle, I ride behind Carson." Jared smirked as he fixed a gaze so heated upon his lover that Pierce had to look away or feel like a voyeur. "I love wrapping my arms around his waist, letting me feel up his sexy chest any time I want."

Sam snorted, shaking his head. His smile caused the scar on his face to crease in an interesting way, giving him a rugged edge. "There are several in our group who ride together, so you won't be alone in that regard." Then his brows furrowed as he swept his gaze up and down his body. "You're a strong-looking human. Why can't you learn to ride?"

Daevon beat Pierce in responding. "First, you can learn anything you set your mind to," he stated firmly. "You have a learning disability. You're not dim."

Pierce sighed as he smiled fondly at Daevon. "It's nice of you to say. I don't say those things because I'm insulting myself. I've accepted my issues." He rubbed his fingertips over the smaller man's jawline. "Can you?" He glanced around at Kontra. "Can your people?"

"Well, first you'd have to tell me what issues you think you have," Kontra replied, picking up his half-eaten sandwich. "Do you wanna sit down and explain everything?" He waved toward the vacant space on the bench opposite him.

As much as Pierce hated having to explain himself and his past, he wanted to be able to give Daevon his desires, too.

That's how a partnership works, right?

After sitting on the bench beside Daevon, Pierce accepted a soda from Mutegi. He popped the cap, then took a sip. After wincing as the fizz tingled his senses, he placed it on the table.

Pierce tapped the can with the forefingers of one hand as he rubbed Daevon's thigh with his other. Appreciating the contact, he drew strength from it. He opened his mouth and slowly explained his past—how his mother had hidden her drug addiction, which damaged his developing brain, not to mention his added dyslexia—and the difficulties that came with it.

Chapter Eight

"I get easily distracted, even while driving. If I don't keep reminding myself to focus, my mind will start to drift. If I were driving a motorcycle and I became distracted, going into the other lane or hitting rumble strips or sliding into a soft berm . . . I could easily wipe out and get hurt. That's why I drive a *Jeep* with roll-bars. I'm just lucky I've always been able to correct when someone honks."

Daevon recalled Pierce's words of explanation as he drove them back to his mate's home. Even with the assurances from the others that they could work around that, his human had just chuckled and waved away their comments. Pierce really did seem to have complete acceptance of how he worked around his issues.

That means I need to accept them, too.

Knowing trying to change his mate wasn't the way to please him, Daevon took a deep breath, then two. He focused on the feel of Pierce's arms around him and how his mate had agreed to put in his two weeks' notice. His human had accepted the idea of traveling, but he wanted to introduce Daevon to his father first.

Never met the parents of a lover before.

For his mate, however, Daevon would do it. Hell, he would pretty much do anything for him. With that thought firmly in mind, Daevon grinned as he pulled to a stop in Pierce's driveway.

"Oh, hey." Daevon gripped Pierce's leg, staying him from moving off the back of his bike. "Did you want to get your

Jeep first?"

Daevon had been so eager to get Pierce to a bed, so they could mate, he'd completely forgotten that they'd left his mate's vehicle at the pub where they'd had lunch.

Pierce chuckled before awkwardly pressing a kiss to Daevon's neck. "Naw. We can do it later." He reached around and blatantly rubbed Daevon's hard cock with one hand while fondling his nipples with the other. "Jared was so right. This is hawt."

Moaning, Daevon shuddered under Pierce's ministrations. When the bike wobbled, he grabbed his mate's hands and pulled them from his body. "Off the bike," Daevon ordered gruffly. "Open the garage. Want you inside, naked and on the bed, ten minutes ago."

Laughing loudly, Pierce swung off the bike. He reached down and blatantly adjusted himself. Then, with a wink, he strutted up to the garage door and punched in a code on the panel set in the left side of the archway. The garage door began to rise, and Pierce bent and swung under it, showing off his tight ass.

Daevon groaned as he started his bike moving forward again. As soon as the door had cleared enough, he ducked his head and headed inside. As he lowered the kickstand and settled the bike, Daevon spotted Pierce slipping through the man-sized door at the back.

After getting off the bike and removing his helmet, Daevon hurried after him. He slapped the button beside the door, causing the garage door to reverse directions, closing behind him. Then he followed Pierce inside, locking the door.

Nearly swallowing his tongue, Daevon barely registered the décor. He noticed Pierce's helmet rested on the kitchen bar, as did his mate's shirt. His human was leaning with his back against the counter, leering at him.

Daevon's brain nearly fizzed out.

Pierce arched a little, displaying his heavily muscled torso beautifully. He'd opened his jeans, showing that he'd gone commando. His right hand was wrapped around his heavy, swollen shaft, and he teased at his beaded nipples with his left.

"B-Bed," Daevon rumbled, his voice deep and gruff with his need. "Where?"

Daevon couldn't remember the last time he'd been reduced to one-word sentences. Need pulsed through his body, and his cock throbbed. Every instinct he had screamed at him to grab his mate's waist, spin him around, and bend him over the counter.

Control. Keep control.

To Daevon's relief, Pierce turned and began sauntering through the living room. With each step he took, his jeans slid down, enticing Daevon with the view. By the time Pierce reached a hallway, his crack and half his ass cheeks were on gorgeous display.

Moaning, Daevon yanked his head out of his ass and hurried after him. In the process, he jerked his polo shirt over his head. Then he unbuttoned his jeans.

When Daevon reached the bedroom, Pierce stood beside the bed. He was bending over, shoving off his sneakers, socks, and jeans. Seeing Pierce's teasing, Daevon growled, his need surging through him.

"Playing with fire, Pierce," Daevon rumbled as he crossed the distance between them. When Pierce straightened and half-turned, giving him a cheeky smile and revealing he was once again jacking his dick, Daevon gave him a narrow-eyed stare. "Cheeky mate."

Daevon didn't give Pierce a chance to respond. Grabbing his mate's slim, muscular hips, he used his shifter strength to lift the much larger man. Upon hearing Pierce's yelp of surprise, Daevon tossed his human onto his bed.

As Daevon watched Pierce bounce once, then roll onto his

back, he bent to remove his boots. Upon seeing his mate's surprised expression and scenting the same, he straightened and leered at his man. "Told you shifters are stronger."

"You weren't kiddin'," Pierce mumbled. Then he swept his gaze over Daevon's frame. "Wow. You're small and pretty, but not your cock. Long and slender." He licked his lips. "Wanna taste you."

Daevon shoved off his jeans, taking his socks with them. "Can't remember when anyone called me pretty," he commented as he crawled onto the bed beside Pierce. "But I'll gladly let you suck my cock anytime you want . . . after we bond."

Pierce nodded, looking eager. He reached over his head and under the pillow. When he pulled his hand back, he held a tube of lube.

"Jacked off to memories of what you talked about last night," Pierce told him roughly, holding it out. "Can't wait to do everything with you."

Anticipation to fulfill his mate's every desire eased Daevon's need to rut, to mate.

Daevon took the offered lube, then crawled between Pierce's spread thighs. His new — and final — lover peered up at him with lust swimming in his eyes. Pierce's eyes were dilated. His cheeks and neck were flushed. Even his lips were parted as he panted softly while he peered at Daevon, his expression one of anticipation and need.

"Gorgeous," Daevon whispered. "You are stunning."

Without waiting for an answer, Daevon opened his mouth, bent over, and swallowed Pierce's thick cock to the root. He utilized his centuries of experience and did as he'd promised on the phone. Swallowing around Pierce's circumcised head, he massaged the flesh with his throat muscles.

A wash of pride flooded Daevon upon hearing Pierce's cry of pleasure. The sound of his bliss echoed off the walls, filling the room. Sucking strongly, he pulled halfway off, allowing him to take a breath.

Then Daevon repeated his ministrations.

While doing that, Daevon used his thumb to pop the cap on the tube. He poured a liberal amount onto the fingers of his right hand, and then he snapped it closed again. Sinking down again, he used his clean hand to cradle Pierce's balls.

Pierce planted his feet and bucked as a scream rent the air.

Daevon accepted Pierce's cock, allowing his lover to bury his erection deep in his throat. At the same time, he felt the orbs he gently fondled and rolled draw up. Reading the signs, Daevon swallowed around his head as he teased his lubed fingertips over Pierce's hole.

That seemed to be the final straw.

Shuddering and moaning, Pierce thrust up once more. His body trembled as his cock throbbed in Daevon's mouth. Pierce's hot cream shot down Daevon's throat, and he quickly swallowed it.

As Daevon shoved his finger into Pierce's channel as deeply as he could, he released Pierce's sack so he could grab his hip. He easily forced his mate's hips flush to the bed, allowing him to ease partway off his dick. His lover's next bursts of seed landed on his tongue, coating his taste buds with his salty, tasty flavor.

Daevon moaned softly, loving that taste. As he continued to suckle lightly, he turned his attention to massaging and tonging at his frenulum. At the same time, Daevon began easing his finger out, then pushed it back in again. He made certain to glance his fingertip over his mate's prostate with each move.

"D-Daevon," Pierce whined, shifting restlessly in his grip. "O-Oh, fuck! Still hard."

After sliding a second finger in beside the first, Daevon allowed Pierce's erection to slip from between his lips. He grinned upon hearing his mate's whine of protest. Ignoring it, he nosed downward, rubbing his chin over his lover's ball sack.

Pierce sucked in a harsh breath.

When Daevon licked over his soft nut sack, Pierce let out a whimpering moan. Grinning to himself, he opened his mouth and began lapping at the lightly furred flesh. As he worked the sensitive skin, reveling in the shudders and moans of his human, Daevon eased a third finger into his chute.

Gods, I love those sounds.

"N-Now," Pierce insisted breathlessly. "I-I want t-to feel you now."

More than willing to move things along—his own balls hung heavy and swollen between his thighs, and his cock throbbed insistently—Daevon hummed . . . while he was still nuzzling his man's balls.

Pierce shuddered again as he ground out, "Hurry. Now, h-hurry."

Daevon lifted and stared down at his human, enjoying the way his prick bobbed so beautifully. "I will always give you what you need, my handsome mate," he crooned as he pulled his fingers from Pierce's chute. "Always."

Even as Pierce gasped harshly, he mumbled, "Want to do the same for you."

Nodding slowly, Daevon realized that was part of why Pierce was doing all this . . . accepting him, letting him fuck him, hell . . . even leaving the town and his only family.

And I will make it all up to him.

And Daevon would start by doing as Pierce wanted . . . needed . . . hell, begged. He would fuck him until he orgasmed a second time. Then he would bite him, complete their bond, and make him come all over again.

"Relax, Pierce," Daevon crooned softly, as he knee-walked forward. "I will always take care of you."

As Daevon held Pierce's gaze, he bent and placed his hand

on the comforter near his lover's shoulder. He gripped his erection with his right and jacked himself, coating himself with the lube still on his palm. His cock twitched in his grip, and he suppressed a shudder as his balls threatened to tighten. Instead, Daevon gripped the base of his erection in a tight grip, stemming his need to come.

Daevon lowered to his forearm as he kissed his cock head to Pierce's stretched hole. He nudged gently, shivering at the feel of his striated muscle sliding over his crown. His erection throbbed, and he sealed his lips over his mate's own.

Then Daevon eased forward.

The feel of Pierce's silky passage opening to him, sliding around him, encasing him, drew a deep groan from him.

Daevon shuddered as Pierce rocked into his push and swallowed the noises he made, welcoming him inside him in more ways than one.

Once Daevon had bottomed out, he paused. It felt as if his eyes rolled to the back of his head. It felt that good . . . amazing . . . exquisite. Lifting his head, he moaned again with the effort it took to stay still, to wait until Pierce's clenching muscles relaxed around his length.

After who the hell knew how long, Daevon felt Pierce's hands stroking up and down his back. He managed to blink open eyes he didn't remember closing. Peering at his flush-faced lover, he tried to find words when his brain was damn near mush.

Pierce smiled at him. "Move, Dae," he urged, wrapping his strong arms around his torso and rubbing up and down his back. "Now." Then his tone took on a husky rumble as he ordered, "Fuck me."

Daevon moaned, and he was helpless to do anything but obey. He did as his mate asked.

Chapter Nine

Pierce had never been so hot to be fucked in his life. His body felt as if it was on fire, and heat sizzled through his veins. His chute muscles fluttered along Daevon's length where it was embedded inside him, and he desperately wanted to feel the long slender shaft rubbing and sliding within him.

When Daevon finally began to move, Pierce's inner nerve endings lit up, sending fire through his groin. It spread swiftly, tingles zinging through him. His balls rolled pleasantly as his cock twitched where it was pinned between their bodies, his pre-cum creating a pleasant glide.

"Oh, god!" Pierce groaned. Gripping the comforter, he arched his back and rocked his hips up into each of Daevon's ruts. "Yeah. More. Please, more."

"Anything for you, my mate," Daevon purred roughly into his ear. "So fucking perfect."

Daevon blanketed Pierce, resting his forehead against Pierce's shoulder. Gripping Pierce's thick thigh, he slammed forward, driving into him, somehow managing to go even deeper. Then he began moving in earnest, pounding into him.

"Dae!" Pierce cried. Lifting his legs higher, he wrapped them around Daevon's waist. "Yeah." Pierce released the comforter in favor of gripping his lover, holding him tight to his chest.

Their bodies slid together, slicked by their sweat as they came together. The sound of skin slapping mixed with their grunts and groans, creating the most erotic cacophony of music Pierce had ever enjoyed. His blood rushed in his ears, and his erection rubbed deliciously against his lover's torso.

"Pierce."

Daevon's voice sounded ragged as he lifted his head and caught his eye. The expression of tortured bliss told Pierce the smaller man was hanging on by a thread. His heart rate spiked, and his own need crested in response.

"Dae," Pierce whispered back, holding Pierce's gaze.

With one more rut where Daevon pegged his gland and rubbed his stomach over Pierce's dick, Pierce's balls pulled tight. He sucked in a harsh gasp, the ecstasy of his orgasm flooding him. Shuddering, he pressed his temple against Daevon's as he moaned and rode out his pleasure.

"Oh, Pierce," Daevon muttered into his ear, freezing with his erection deep inside him.

Pierce smiled. "Yeah, breed me."

In the next second, Pierce vaguely recognized the warmth of Daevon's seed as he felt the dick in his chute twitch and pulse. He hummed at the unfamiliar sensation. Rubbing his hands up and down Daevon's back, he grinned. He loved knowing his body had given his lover so much pleasure.

Daevon lifted his head and smiled back at him. "Ready for orgasm number three?"

Chuckling, Pierce lifted his brows. "Three? Not sure that's possible for a little while, even as sexy as you are." He already felt his prick softening.

"You will." Daevon winked as he lowered his head and began mouthing kisses along Pierce's neck and shoulder. "Enjoy."

Pierce tipped his head to the side a little, enjoying Daevon's post-coital ministrations. "Mmmm . . . that feels nice."

Daevon chuckled again. "This will feel even better."

Before Pierce could come up with a response, Daevon bit

him. He gasped at the spike of pain from sharp teeth breaking his flesh. Even as he began to cry out in pain, wondering why Pierce thought he would enjoy being bitten, the sensation changed.

Pierce shouted Daevon's name as bliss caused white spots to dance across his vision. His nipples beaded anew, and his cock thickened once more. Then the strange warm sensation centered in his balls, and he cried out as, just as Daevon had promised, another orgasm hit him.

Blind-sided, Pierce allowed his arms and legs to flop back to the bed. He tipped his head back and moaned roughly, shuddering with the sensations pouring through his body. Each time Daevon sucked on his neck, it seemed to transfer straight to his cock, and Pierce kept coming and coming.

His eyes rolled back, and with a smile on his face, Pierce passed out from bliss.

Pierce hummed as he roused, enjoying the feel of the hand rubbing over his chest. Turning his head, he pried his eyelids open. He took in his sexy lover lying beside him.

Daevon rested on his side, his head propped on his elbow. His brows were furrowed, putting a little crease between them. Worry filled his dark eyes.

"Hey, what's wrong?" Pierce asked as he slid his left arm under Daevon's torso. He tugged him closer, causing him to half flop on his body. "C'mere."

"Not wrong," Daevon assured, tracing the grooves of Pierce's abdominals with his fingertips. "Just worried about you." Resting his head on Pierce's shoulder, he stared up at him. "As ego-boosting as making you pass out from pleasure can be, I was worried I'd hurt you, too. You were out for a good ten minutes."

Pierce waggled his brows at Daevon. "You can make me pass out from pleasure anytime." Relieved to see his lover's tension ease as he settled against him, Pierce sighed. *God, I have a lover.* Chuckling softly, Pierce mumbled, "Wow. That Jared guy was right." He squeezed Daevon tighter against him as he used his right hand to cradle his jaw and urge his chin up. "Never cuddled before. This is nice."

Then Pierce sealed his lips over Daevon's and thrust his tongue into his mouth. His lover immediately allowed him entrance. He explored languidly, mapping his teeth and gums.

Over the next few hours, they did some of that necking they'd talked about at the restaurant, and Pierce explored Daevon's body, using his hands, lips, teeth, and tongue to drive his shifter out of his mind.

Pierce danced left, easily evading his opponent's punch. Striking out, he landed a hook to the other man's ear, making him rock sideways. He followed that with a combination to his torso, driving him back.

The man bounced off the ropes and came back swinging, a determined scowl twisting his features.

Pivoting to the right, Pierce blocked. He bit back a grunt as he felt the man connect a punch to his ribs. When Pierce's opponent pressed what he thought was his advantage, he saw his opening.

Pierce accepted another hit, this one higher on his chest. Then he dodged the shot the man aimed at his head. Stepping close as he swung his own fist, he struck the guy's temple. The other boxer stumbled, giving Pierce time to nail him again.

Watching his opponent fall to the ground, Pierce took a step backward and danced on his toes. His adrenaline surged as he waited for the other man to rise. He shook out his arms while the referee knelt next to the man and began counting.

The guy only managed to make it to his hands and knees by the time the ref reached ten. As the ref rose and gripped

Pierce's wrist, lifting his arm in the air and announcing him the winner of the bout, the other fighter's trainer and assistant ducked between the ropes. They helped the other man up while Anthony entered the ring and patted Pierce on the back.

After listening to the cheers of the crowd for a few minutes, the referee released Pierce. He followed Anthony out of the ring, glancing around and searching for Daevon's slender frame. Anthony gripped his bicep, and leading him away from the ring, he drew Pierce's attention.

When Pierce realized they weren't headed to the locker room, he asked, "Where we headed? What's up?"

"My office," Anthony told him. "I thought you might want a few minutes of quiet after your fight."

"But shouldn't I get cleaned up?"

Pierce had told Daevon to meet him in the locker room if he couldn't get near him after the fight. His lover had explained that, since his shifter instincts were to keep him safe, he couldn't be too close while Pierce was fighting. While Daevon was in the crowd, he had to be fairly far away . . . and in the presence of other shifters who could keep him from trying to get into the ring and beating the shit out of whoever Pierce was fighting.

Between learning about that issue and having his strength increase due to bonding with Daevon, Pierce knew this would be his last competition. He couldn't say he was upset by that. His training had always been more for stress and energy release.

"Yeah, but you have time," Anthony countered, reaching the door to his office and unlocking it. The man kept it locked when so many extra people crowded into the gym to witness a boxing match. "Come in here a minute."

Pierce obeyed, following Anthony into his office. The space wasn't large, but his friend kept it meticulously clean. He crossed the room, aiming for the plastic chair in front of the desk as he heard Anthony shut the door.

Before Pierce reached it, Anthony gripped his hips. Stilling, he peered over his shoulder, questions filling him. Did he already have a bruise forming from where the guy he'd been fighting had nailed his upper back?

Just as Pierce opened his mouth to question him, he felt Anthony's hands slide forward. He skimmed his palms over his abdominals . . . then down. When he began dipping his fingers under the waistband of Pierce's shorts, Pierce snapped out of his shock.

Jerking forward, Pierce yanked away from Anthony. He spun, his still-gloved hands lifting. "Whoa. What are you doing?" Even as he asked the question, he realized his occasional fuck-buddy's intention had been kind of clear.

Damn.

Something like this happening had certainly never occurred to him.

Anthony offered a heated smile as he moved toward him again. "I woulda thought that would be obvious, even to you, Pierce." He waggled his brows. "You have a good hour before you're to take on the winner of the fight going on right now. Let me help you down from that adrenaline rush you always get."

It was true. Pierce normally ended up with a semi while boxing. Except, Anthony had never offered to help him out with it before at the gym. They'd always met up at one of their homes at a pre-arranged time, and the last time had been a month before.

Then some of Anthony's words snagged his attention. "Obvious even to me?" He sighed. Anthony had never seemed to have a problem with his difficulties before. "Not nice, man."

Daevon had always insisted there was nothing wrong with him, and his lover appreciated him just as he was.

My lover.

"I didn't mean it like that," Anthony stated, looking a little chagrined. "Sorry, Pierce." Then he grinned again and glanced down at his crotch. "Thinking with my dick made me thoughtless." Anthony's focus slid to Pierce's groin, and he beckoned. "Why don't you let me suck you to full hardness, then I'll bend over my desk for you." Rubbing his fly, he stated huskily, "You were fierce in that ring, man. Turned me on."

Shaking his head, Pierce told his buddy, "Uh, no thanks, Anth." He saw the way Anthony's brows shot up, his surprise evident. "I'm actually seeing someone, so, um... I can't screw around with you or, or anyone else now." Pierce began pulling off his gloves as he continued, "His name is Daevon, and he's out there in the crowd. I was supposed to meet him in the locker room, so I better go."

"Wow," Anthony murmured, taking a step backward as he rubbed his palm over his face. "Never thought the day would come when you got serious about someone."

"Really? Why?" Pierce moved past Anthony, who shoved his hands into his pockets. "Because most people think I'm slow?"

Anthony laughed, shaking his head. "Naw, man." He slapped him on the back as Pierce unlocked the door. As he pulled it open and headed out, Anthony followed and stated, "You're a great guy. Friendly. Fun. Honest. Any guy would be damn fucking lucky to have you." He shrugged as he closed and relocked his office. "I just never thought you were the settling down type. Like me."

"Oh." Pierce grinned broadly as pleasure filled him. "Thanks, man."

Nodding, Anthony bumped him with his shoulder. "Go get your man, buddy."

Pierce nodded. Still grinning, he headed to the locker room to do just that.

Chapter Ten

After building their bond for a week, only separating when Pierce had to work, watching his lover box was damn difficult for Daevon. His wolverine wanted to leap into the ring and claw out the guy's eyes he was fighting. That was why he sat in the back . . . with several of Kontra's men surrounding him.

The warthog shifter, Mutegi, relaxed in a chair next to him, his arm around his human mate, Ben. On Daevon's other side sat Payson, a hyena shifter. His mate Land had declined to come, saying boxing didn't interest him. Instead, the human had gone grocery shopping with a few other guys.

The pack's doctor, Eli, as well as his wolf shifter mate, Sam, had come as well. Eli had insisted that he could check Pierce over between bouts. He'd explained how it would help ease Daevon's wolverine.

So far, the python shifter had been right, too. They'd checked in on Pierce after his first bout, and he'd been declared fine. Pierce had assured Daevon that he was, but hearing the doctor confirm it had settled his mind.

"He's good," Payson commented, grinning widely. "Just knocked that dude out."

Listening to the cheers, Daevon nodded absently. His mate was good at boxing. He seemed to find a zone and intensity that the other men were missing.

Daevon guessed it was in part due to the way his brain worked just a little differently than others.

A couple of hours later, Daevon watched with pride filling him as Pierce was announced the winner. He stood and clapped and cheered along with many others. Spotting Bill standing off to the side with Stan and another buddy who had a cast on his hand, Daevon recognized the look of hatred and disgust on the trio's faces.

Stan had been knocked out in his first fight. Bill had been disqualified in his second fight. Daevon guessed the third guy hadn't fought because of the cast on his left hand.

Homophobes.

Daevon dismissed the bastards and headed toward the locker room. Once again, Eli and Sam accompanied him inside. While Anthony had appeared surprised by the presence of the doctor and nurse pair, Pierce had smoothed it over by assuring the gym owner his dad had insisted.

Finding Pierce standing in the far locker room aisle, Daevon offered him a wide grin. "Congratulations, my mate," he rumbled as he drew closer.

Daevon rested his hands on his bulging pectorals and stood on his tip-toes. Pleasure filled him when Pierce dipped his head and welcomed his kiss, gripping his hips and holding him steady. When Daevon broke the lip-lock, the scent of arousal perfumed the air . . . and it wasn't all his own.

"Damn, you can kiss," Daevon whispered, chuckling huskily.

"Thanks." Pierce winked as he slid one hand up and rubbed his thumb along the curve of Daevon's lips. "Never really enjoyed it much until you."

Pleasure filled Daevon at the compliment. He opened his mouth to answer, but Eli stepped forward. "Would you like me to check him over real quick?" His dark eyes were full of mirth as he teased, "Or should I leave it to you . . . after you take him back to your place to fuck him into the mattress?"

Sam snickered from where he stood next to Eli, and the tall, slender python shifter wrapped his arm around his shoulders and tucked him against him.

"God, so fuckin' disgusting," a nasty voice commented from behind them. "You fags need to be taught a lesson, and since I couldn't do it in the ring, here's good enough."

Turning, Daevon wasn't the least bit surprised to see Bill, Stan, and the third man. Even though his left hand was in a cast, he held a short baton in his right. The other pair were cracking their knuckles, clearly threatening.

"Oh good grief," Daevon grumbled, rolling his eyes.

"I would rethink your course of action if I were you," Eli commented as he used his hand on Sam's shoulder to maneuver his mate behind him. "This will only get you hurt."

Daevon knew Sam, while a wolf shifter, was submissive. If push came to shove, he wasn't certain if the man could fight. Then Sam gripped Eli's upper arm and slipped around to stand next to him.

Huh. Guess having a mate threatened would do it.

"Well, we ain't you, are we?" Bill replied, obviously the ringleader. "We're gonna bust you four up, then go take out your three friends." He cackled, sounding like a demented fool, before adding, "Seven less fags in the world. Hell yeah."

"You really think the three of you can take us?" Pierce asked, stepping forward to stand next to Daevon.

Stan smirked as he swept his gaze over them. "A doctor, two twinks, and an exhausted boxer. Oh, yeah." Then he reached into his back pocket—Bill did the same—and both men pulled out a set of brass knuckles and slipped them on. "And just to give us an even bigger advantage." Stan snickered cruelly.

Eli's expression was wry as he glanced Daevon's way. "Idiot homophobes. Wanna take bets on how swiftly they go down?" His eyes darkened with malice as he added, "I'll take mine out with one charge. Head slammed into the lockers."

"I'll take mine with two punches," Daevon claimed, rolling his shoulders to loosen his limbs. He caught Pierce's eye. "We can handle this, if you want to sit and relax." Then he voice turned to a husky growl. "My wolverine would really like you out of this."

Pierce grinned widely, his brown eyes beginning to twinkle. "All right." He took a step back and settled on one of the benches situated in the aisle between the lockers. "If Sam doesn't mind taking out Kenny, I'll just wait right here."

Sam growled low in his throat, the sound very wolf-like. His dark eyes blazed with anger as he clenched his black hands. "I'm gonna put him over that bench and spank his ass with his own baton like a naughty schoolboy."

Daevon and the others laughed.

The trio of homophobes charged.

Daevon allowed Bill to swing at him, and he easily dodged. After having watched him in the ring, he'd learned his tells. The man led with his left shoulder just before he was going to swing his right arm.

Smashing his fist into Bill's side, Daevon grinned ferally upon hearing him grunt and seeing him stumble sideways. He followed that with a jab to Bill's jaw. Remembering to temper his shifter strength at the last second, he pulled his punch just a smidge.

Bill still went down like a sack of potatoes.

As Daevon watched the human fall, he heard a crash. Turning, he spotted Eli doing just as he'd said. The python shifter slammed Stan's head into a locker, and the human crumpled to the ground.

"Just because we're small and gay doesn't mean we're weak," Sam declared right before the sound of smacking reached Daevon's ears. "You're a bad man, and you're gonna get what you deserve when we press charges."

Daevon didn't know how Sam had done it, but he'd done exactly as he'd threatened. The little black man had the much larger human draped over one of the center benches. He had his left hand on his back between his shoulder blades, his right hand held the baton, and his right leg was stuck between his legs so he couldn't rise again.

Sam even swatted him several times on the ass with the baton.

Chuckling, Eli crossed to his mate as he pulled his belt from around his hips. "Let's get him tied up. Then we'll call the police."

"I already called Sheriff Stillwell," Pierce claimed from where he still sat on the bench. "He has Deputy Miller on the way. We need to stick around until she gets here so she can take our statements."

"All right." Daevon returned to his lover's side.

"That'll give us enough time for me to check you over real quick," Eli claimed, joining them. He knelt and started inspecting his rib cage. "Does anything hurt anywhere?"

Daevon sat next to Pierce, holding his hand, as Eli verified that he was well. When the man was done and moved away, he lifted his mate's hand to his lips. After kissing the knuckles, earning a smile from his human, Daevon wrapped his arm around him.

Pierce returned the move, and they sat quietly, waiting patiently.

The pounding on a door caught their attention. "Hey! Open up!"

"Oh. That's Anthony," Pierce stated, pushing to his feet. "They must have locked the locker room door when they came in."

"You good with them?" Daevon asked Eli and Sam, who were watching their attackers—two unconscious and one awake and glaring mutinously.

Eli smirked. "Of course."

Daevon followed Pierce, unwilling to let him out of his sight after all the fighting. "Why didn't you insist on fighting with me?" he asked curiously as he slid his hand into Pierce's, twining their fingers.

Pierce shrugged as he squeezed them. "You said you wanted me to sit it out. Why would I insist?"

"Pride," Daevon replied instantly. Meeting Pierce's gaze, he admitted, "Most big guys who just won the boxing tournament . . . well—" Pausing, Daevon tried to think of a polite way to finish that.

"Aww . . . I don't need to prove myself like that." Pierce paused beside the locked door, but he didn't unlock it. Instead, he pulled Daevon into his arms and leveled a serious stare at him. "I want you happy, too, Daevon. That goes both ways." Then Pierce grinned and waggled his eyebrows. "And it's a good thing I'm not like most big guys."

"I love that you're not like other big guys," Daevon replied, rubbing his hands up and down his human's huge arms. "You're perfect just the way you are."

Pierce beamed at him, then dipped his head and sealed their mouths together, stealing Daevon's breath away.

A long moment later, the pounding on the door started again, breaking them apart.

Laughing, Pierce released him and unlocked it. Not only did Anthony stand there, but so did two deputies—one male and one female.

Daevon intended to make the explanations as short and sweet as possible, because as he held Pierce's hand and led the group back toward where Eli and Sam waited with their attackers, Daevon knew he had something much more important to be doing.

I'm going to take my human home and love up every inch of his magnificent body. Then I'll hold his kind heart for as long as the fates allow.

Daevon thought that sounded like a damn fine idea.
Inspired by the Fates.
Oh yeah.

You may also enjoy the following from eXtasy Books Inc:

Vying for His Affection
Charlie Richards

Excerpt

Rhyme had never scented blood so enticing. His stomach clenched, and his mouth watered. Need for the man before him caused his half-hard dick to thicken so fast Rhyme nearly swayed on his feet.

Gods! Could this human be my beloved?

"Oh, little bit," Rhyme mumbled. "Let's go for a moonlight ride."

"Really? What the hell makes you think I'd go anywhere alone with you?" the man snapped, resting his hands on his hips. "First you insult me, twice, and now you think I'm gonna give you the time of day?" He snorted as he turned away from him, then sauntered toward Murdoch. "Looks like you got a little pony ready for me, handsome." He stopped before the animal and eyed it somewhat warily. "What's its name?"

Rhyme's stomach clenched for a whole new reason. He hated being dismissed . . . but he hated the upset scent rolling off the sexy man even more. The human who could very well be his beloved had thought he'd been insulting him.

Shit!

When Murdoch glanced Rhyme's way, a question flashing in his eyes, Rhyme mouthed, Name? His friend and fellow vampire offered an almost infinitesimal nod before turning his attention to the human.

"This is Lily," Murdoch told him, rubbing the mare's nose. "And she's not really a pony. She's just small for a quarter horse." Holding out his hand, he added, "What's your name?"

"I'm tired of people making fun of my size," the man stated, ignoring the question and petting the horse's neck. "You're a pretty girl, Lily. Are you a nice girl?"

"She is a nice girl," Murdoch assured. "And we pulled her out to make you more comfortable, not to make fun of you." He offered a reassuring smile as he added, "We do the same for all our guests." Pointing at a huge behemoth of a man, Murdoch told him, "Just like our friend over there is paired up with that gelding on the end."

Rhyme watched the human's eyes widen as he took in the size of the horse Murdoch had pointed out. Charlie was a seventeen-hand gelding who was part quarter horse and part friesian. They'd ended up with the animal when one of their bigger mares slipped through a broken fence and got into the pen with Gypsum's stallion. The resulting foal ended up big. Fortunately, he'd been born with his mother's sweet disposition.

"You all put your foot in it," a young woman stated from where she'd stopped beside Rhyme. She smirked at him as she held out her hand. "I'm Lilibeth. Which horse is mine?"

"It wasn't intentional," Rhyme muttered, feeling his cheeks warm. Good thing his dark skin hid such things. After a quick glance over Lilibeth's frame, he pointed toward the gelding next to Lily. "That's Jake. He's a nice boy."

"You did not just check me out," Lilibeth said with narrowed eyes.

Rhyme barked a laugh as he shook his head. "No, ma'am," he immediately assured her. "Just verifying leg length and body type so I can put you in a comfortable saddle."

Lilibeth nodded, her stance relaxing. "Okay." Then she headed toward the horse Rhyme had indicated.

Over the next several minutes, Rhyme and Murdoch went through the process of assigning horses and getting everyone comfortable in the saddle. When Murdoch moved toward the little guy at the end to finish the process, Rhyme gripped his upper arm, staying the action. "This one's mine," he murmured upon seeing the fellow vampire's surprise.

"You sure?" his friend muttered back. "Doesn't seem to want much to do with you."

"I'll have to fix that, then, won't I?" Rhyme didn't extrapolate. There wasn't time. "Start the usual spiel."

Murdoch nodded and headed toward the front of the group, not questioning him again. As a lower-ranking enforcer for their vampire coven, his buddy wouldn't question him. Murdoch would follow Rhyme's orders.

"I'm sorry you thought I was making fun of you," Rhyme stated after stopping next to the man on Lily. He rested his hand on his knee and squeezed lightly. "It wasn't my intention."

The human peered down at him with narrowed eyes. "How else should I have taken being called the little stringbean?" There was a snarl in his tenor voice. "Get your hand off me."

Rhyme grimaced as he lifted his hands in placation. "Okay. You're right. That was thoughtless of me." Scowling at his memory of their first meeting, he grumbled, "And you called me oversized, so I don't know if you have any room to talk. I'm only six-foot-two."

"With a giant frame," the man pointed out, stabbing his finger in the air at his torso. "Wide shoulders, big pecs. I bet you even have a six-pack under there. Anyway, it doesn't matter. Just adjust my stirrups and let's get on with this bullshit company activity."

Swallowing hard, Rhyme tried to figure out what he could say to mend the rift that his overheard comment had created. *If he's my beloved, shouldn't the pull to bond be working in his favor?* He'd seen it happen with other vampires.

Doing as the man had ordered, Rhyme swiftly adjusted the length of the stirrups to a more comfortable position for him. Once he was done, he couldn't resist gripping his calf and helping him get his foot in the stirrup. He squeezed lightly along the skinny calf, rubbing his thumb over the faint muscle.

"Damn, you're skinny." The words were out of Rhyme's mouth before he could stop them. All his focus was on touching the slender man on the horse before him and how it made his blood burn and thud through his veins. "So fucking—"

"Shut the fuck up," the human snarled, jerking his foot away from Rhyme's hand. "I said get your hands off me."

In the process, the man slammed his heel into Lily's side. The mare jerked and shifted sideways, instantly responding to the unexpected pressure. She didn't have far to go, considering Jake stood next to her.

Still, it was enough.

The man lost his balance and tumbled toward Rhyme, squeaking in alarm. On instinct, he caught the human. As luck would have it, the man knocked Rhyme's hat from his head with his flailing limbs, then slammed one palm into his face and the other to his shoulder.

Rhyme couldn't help but gasp, which caused his fang to scrape over the human's palm. The man's blood oozed from the scratch, filling his mouth. The sweet metallic taste caused Rhyme's vampiric instincts to flare to life as his entire body surged with hunger.

Mine!

"Let go of me, goddammit!"

Coming back to himself with a mental thud, Rhyme realized that he was holding his sweet beloved around his waist. He had his face tucked against the man's neck, and he was inhaling his scent. Rhyme even rubbed his right hand up and down his near leg, since the other one was still draped over the saddle.

Lily had calmed. Probably thanks to Murdoch, who stood at her head, rubbing her nose. His fellow vampire stared at him quizzically.

Unable to explain right then, Rhyme settled his beloved, the human he hoped to soon make his forever bonded love, back into the saddle. It took every damn scrap of self-control he had to release him.

As Rhyme nodded at Murdoch and joined him before the group, he prayed his aching erection wasn't noticeable, since his flannel over-shirt was untucked. As he listened to his fellow vampire start the instruction spiel they gave every time they took a group on a trail ride, one thought reverberated through his mind.

I met my beloved, and I don't even know his name.

About the Author

Charlie started writing fantasy when she was eight, and after stumbling onto her first erotic romance at age nineteen, she realized her true calling. She now focuses on writing gay erotic romance, normally of the paranormal variety, with heroes of all kinds. With the help and support of her husband, Charlie finally fulfilled one of her life-long goals . . . move to acreage with her horses. You can often find her curled up with her laptop and a cup of tea or glass of wine, creating her next adventure. Charlie enjoys exploring the mountains of her new Oregon home on horseback, 4-wheeler, or motorcycle.

She can be reached at ch.richards2010@yahoo.com
Or visit her at www.charlie-richards.com

Printed in Great Britain
by Amazon